A HANDFUL
OF MEN

Also by Robert Wilder:

WALK WITH EVIL

A HANDFUL OF MEN

Robert Wilder

WILDSIDE PRESS

Chapter One

Within the shale-cluttered pass there was no sound, no movement. Strung out in a single line, the fifteen men sat their drooping mounts as though they had been sculptured in relief from the canyon's walls. Their eyes moved up and over the granite rim, searching to find what they knew must be hidden there looking down upon them, watching and waiting for some small sign of indecision or panic. Each man, in his own way, measured the situation and decided how the danger would be met if and when the threat resolved itself into a sudden attack.

Abruptly, from the top of a shining butte in the wavy distance, a puff of black smoke twisted itself into a sinister ball and hung there against the shimmering curtain of sky.

Sullivan Carter, wrists crossed upon the pommel of his saddle, stared at the sooty smoke and then blew softly between dirt-encrusted lips. He turned to the man behind him.

"What do you make of it, Park?"

Parker Manning shook his head and managed a small grin. "You got a piece of paper that says you're the captain, Sul. That means you do the thinkin'."

"I guess a man's a real fool to learn to read, then." The words were softly accented and a small light of amusement showed in his grey eyes as Carter continued to study the ominous sign in the sky. "They've been picking us up and handing us along ever since we came into the pass. If they were going to hit us it seems they would have done it before now."

Manning dug his fingers into a sweat-soaked shirt pocket and withdrew a soggy twist of tobacco. His teeth bit cleanly through the plug and he began to work the chew ruminatively within the dry cavity of his mouth. "Who can figure an Indian?" he said finally. "When he wants to fight, a thousand men won't stop him. When he don't feel like mixin' it up you can't prod him into it. I once rode right through a Kiowa war party an' no one even looked sideways at me. Whenever you do somethin' that ain't normal to their way of thinkin' it confuses them some. By the time they got it figured out maybe you're away."

Sul nodded. There was a faint creak of leather as he turned in the saddle and looked back along the line of riders. They were waiting for him to make the move, reach the decision. They were trapped and they knew it. Now it was up to the Indians. Sul experienced a fierce pride as he glanced over his men. They wore no uniforms. Few even bothered to pin the encircled star of office to their shirts. Yet, they were the law as Texas knew it. The Rangers, recruited from as many different States as there were men in the company. They were judge, jury and executioner. For a thousand miles along the tortuous course of the Rio Grande they pitted themselves against a predatory assortment of cutthroats, highwaymen, thieves, rustlers, marauding bandit gangs sweeping across the border from Mexico, ordinary drunks and trouble makers and the savagely resentful Indians. A handful of men. A miserable handful of men, he thought, who carried themselves as though they were legion. Their clothing was nondescript, picked up casually on the counters of frontier general stores. Here and there a spot of color showed where a bright scarf was twisted to serve as a belt. Only in their manner was there a uniformity. There was confidence in the way they moved; the sure knowledge of how the job was done, the conviction that they were better men. Every recruit had been told the story of a riot in Brownsville to which a single Ranger was sent. "Only one Ranger?" they asked. The classic reply had been, "You've only got one riot, ain't you?"

Sul studied the faces of his men. Young men, all save one, they had a lean resiliency, a studied indifference to fatigue or danger. Men rarely grew old in the Rangers.

Sometimes they didn't even have time to grow up. The exception in the company behind him was "Pop" Warner, a grizzled, scholarly wanderer who had come to Texas from one of the New England states and brought with him the deceptively mild manner of a disillusioned schoolteacher. "Pop" eyed Sul now with the mournful expression of a hound. Then his eyes twinkled and he nodded almost imperceptibly as though to say: Go ahead, boy, whatever you decide is all right with us. Sul smiled and turned away from his inspection.

"I figure we'll go on." He spoke quietly to Manning. "Maybe that's what they don't expect, counting on us trying to make a run for it back the way we came."

Manning shrugged indifferently. "If they're goin' to whack into us they'll do it whether we're goin' forward or backward."

"Drop on back and pass the word as you go. I don't want anyone to lay a hand on his gun unless we get shot at first. We're going to ride slowly, pretending they aren't there and we aren't here." As Park wheeled out of line, Sul called after him. "Send young Carey Latham up here with me. I promised his old man I'd look after him the best I could."

Park hesitated, as though to reply, then changed his mind and rode down the line speaking to each man, motioning a carbine back into its saddle scabbard, cautioning, relaying Carter's instructions.

Sul nudged his horse and then allowed the animal to pick its way at a walk. From the corner of his eye he caught the brief glint of sunlight on metal high on the rocky ledge. At another spot a shadow moved. The muscles over his flat belly contracted as though squeezed by a giant hand. This, he thought, is the way I'd do it if I were an Indian. I'd close in from behind to block a retreat, cork up the other end of the pass and let them have it from the canyon's top and sides. He wondered where they had come from. The pass had been scouted carefully. When Cheever, Griggs and Marker had reported no Indian signs, he had decided to take the pass rather than force the additional twenty miles it would have taken to go around the canyon to reach the settlement of Davis and their headquarters.

A horse and rider moved up into position beside him and Sul barely nodded, wondering at his instinctive dislike of young Latham.

"Manning said you wanted me up here." Oddly enough, the youth made the statement sound like a boast. "We goin' after them Indians?"

"There aren't any Indians as far as we are concerned right now." Sul's voice was level, his eyes on an abrupt angle ahead.

"What's that there smoke then—grandma makin' biscuits?" Latham snickered at his wit and cut a sidelong glance at Carter. "I always heard tell that a dozen Rangers was as good as a hundred Indians."

Sul shook off his irritation. There was an infuriating quality about the youth; the empty speech and manner of a braggart, the idiotic yapping of a mongrel from a point of safety. He wondered if Latham realized that sudden death lurked along each yard of this pass. With an effort he nodded.

"I've heard that, too." He replied agreeably. "Only there's been no evidence that the Indians believe it."

They rode for a few minutes without speaking. Behind them the file strung out, moving slowly, warily. It wasn't likely that the watching Indians would let them escape. Driven, harried, goaded by the constant pressure of the white man, the savages killed and pillaged whenever and wherever they could. They struck at the lonely ranch house, the inadequately guarded wagon train, the small, defenseless settlements. The Rangers could only pursue, punishing the innocent and guilty alike.

Yet, Sul wryly admitted to himself, the Indians were only a small segment of the trouble that beset Texas. The State had become a haven for the lawless. Renegade and Indian teamed up when it suited their purpose and fled across the border when retaliation was threatened. The Federal troops, far too few, could not go beyond this side of the Rio Grande. Only the Rangers sometimes went into Mexico, and this was done without authority. There they were fired upon by those they hunted and by the Mexican *Federales*; the latter furiously contesting any invasion of their country by the hated *Tejans*.

"This is sure a funny way to hunt Indians." Latham broke the silence, unable to resist the pleasure he found in the sound of his own voice.

Sul half-turned to regard him wonderingly. He shook his head wearily. "Try to get it through your head, Latham, that right now we're not hunting Indians. They're hunting us. There's a real good chance that none of us will get out of here alive. If you've got any breath to spare you'd better save it for running. Whatever you see, pretend it isn't there and keep your hands away from that rifle. That's an order."

Latham cackled, cocking his head wisely. "You're spooked, ain't you? No one is goin' to believe that the great Captain Sul Carter got his hair up over some stinkin' Indians he couldn't even see."

Sul wondered dismally at the twisted luck that had sent Latham to his company. The boy, just turned twenty, was an offensive pup, insolent behind his badge and obsequious in the face of a reprimand or an unexpected challenge. He had watched Latham's arrogance with growing concern. The star which they had given him in Austin was not a badge of responsibility but a license to kick an unoffending Indian or one of the humble Mexicans in the settlement of Davis. There wasn't a man in the company he could call a friend. They were suspicious of him, knowing him instinctively for a coward and bully. Often Sul had found himself in the uncomfortable position of defending Latham. As a recruit, he was an obligation Carter could not ignore. So he made excuses, knowing they had a ring of hollowness. Latham was young. He came of doubtful stock. His father, Rale, was a shiftless, bitter man, filled with envy of those who succeeded where he had failed. The parent's character was reflected in the son. Sul would have liked to have Latham transferred but an inflexible sense of duty kept him from making the request. Latham was his job. He smiled inwardly. I'll make a Ranger of him if it kills me. And it might do just that.

Ahead, a small rock suddenly broke away from the high wall, bounced and clattered down into the bed. Instinctively, Sul checked his mount, sucked in his breath. His eyes searched across the rim. Had the stone been dislodged by a careless foot or had it fallen of its own accord? He could feel a swift current of tension run through the line. He understood that each man was holding himself with an almost unbearable effort. Every instinct cried out to put spur to horse and make a dash through the final length of the pass. Yet, they all knew that to run would bring the attack. The spectacle of the Rangers in flight would brew an irresistible excitement in the watching Indians. They would react as a dog would to a running cat. He nudged his mount again and moved forward and after a moment he was aware of the steady clop of hooves on the granite floor, the rasp of leather and the faint tinkle of metal as the column followed.

He cursed to himself with silent fury. What were they waiting for? He knew the answer. This was a sport. The Indians were enjoying themselves. They had their quarry trapped and could dispose of it in their own way after they had savored the full satisfaction of the moment. A hundred or more black, agate eyes must be looking down upon them with glittering pleasure.

A tiny muscle near his jawline leaped convulsively as Sul saw the Indian. He stood there, high on a narrow ledge, his face a hideous smudge of black beneath the traditional war paint. Cradled in the arms crossed over his chest was a rifle. He did not move nor indicate he was even aware of the Rangers below. There was a scornful pride in his bearing. His face was set toward the southern rim of the canyon. Not by a glance would he admit the presence of the Rangers below.

"You see what I do?" Latham's voice squeaked with excitement.

"Just keep riding." Sul did not turn, his eyes on the winding path ahead.

"He's askin' for it. If you don't want him I do." The

carbine's report was a cracking explosion within the walls and the heat of the explosion was a searing blast across Sul's face. Latham had fired before Sul was aware that he had snatched the rifle from his scabbard.

On the ledge the Indian jerked half around as though someone had shoved his shoulder roughly. Then he leaned backward, the rifle spinning from outflung arms, and he came down in a lazy somersault, the body making one complete turn before it landed with an empty thud.

"You fool!" With a sweeping blow Sul's hand cracked savagely across Latham's grinning mouth. "That's ripped it wide open."

As though they were puppets activated by a single string, the figures of Indians jumped into naked silhouette on both sides of the canyon. They fired as they rose, and there was the singing whine of ricochetting bullets and the soft, feathered whisper of arrows. A horse screamed in pain-maddened fear and two Rangers bent tiredly in their saddles and dropped to the ground beneath the threshing hooves. Then the column was in thundering flight. There was no time for heroics, no defiant last stand. They rode hell-for-leather, flattening themselves to their plunging mounts. They ran without shame, knowing that their only hope for survival lay in gaining the mouth of the pass before the Indians streamed down to seal it off. They fired as they rode, emptying revolvers which grew hot in their hands. They fired, not because they expected to hit a target from the pitching back of a horse but only to provide a temporary cover. There was a deep rolling thunder in the canyon, the flying beat of hooves and the crackle of gunfire from above and below. The Indians erupted from their places of concealment as they threw themselves upon their ponies, screaming fury and vengeance at the desperately riding Rangers.

Sul didn't attempt to look back. He knew his men. They would need no orders. The deadly race was to the canyon's entrance where the walls sloped gently down from the top, affording a natural descent for the Indians paralleling them on both sides. Dimly, above the staccato clatter of small arms, the coyote-like yelping of the Indians, he heard a man scream, a sound of agony that clotted in the throat and died abruptly. He felt his own horse plunge, its legs buckle, and he braced himself for the fall but the animal held its footing. A riderless horse came abreast and remained at his side. It dragged the almost shapeless bundle of what had been a man, one foot caught in the whipping stirrup. The body was being beaten into a bloody pulp. Sul emptied his revolver into the animal and watched as it skidded in death, the fall twisting the imprisoned foot from the stirrup. The body was a mangled heap as the surviving Rangers streamed past.

Then, miraculously, the canyon opened up and they were out and into the plain as the first of the Indians began the descent from above. They weren't safe here, either, if the savages continued the pursuit. But as he rode, lashing at his foundering horse, Sul heard the Indians' shouts receding as they began to draw up. Unable to close the pass they were satisfied with the day's kill. Ranging themselves in a wide crescent, they yelled a triumphant defiance at the retreating Rangers who drove their weary bodies and exhausted animals toward the comparative safety of the shimmering prairie.

When it was certain that the Indians would make no attempt to follow beyond the canyon Sul drooped in the saddle, head bent, pain clouding his shadowed eyes. The men moved up from the disorganized file and fanned out in a single front. Slowly, Sul raised his head, glancing to right and left, counting as his eyes swept over them. Ten left out of fifteen. Five men lost in five agonizing minutes. He couldn't even be sure that those who had been left had died quickly and he shut his mind to the thought of a Ranger, wounded and calling out for help in his lonely agony, waiting for the slow torture which would come when the Indians doubled back to pick up their victims.

It was his fault. He shouldn't have risked the pass. But even as he told himself this, he knew it wasn't true. He had taken every precaution. There hadn't been a sign of hostile Indians when they moved into the canyon. They had traversed the same route dozens of times before. Still, he blamed himself. He hadn't been willing to back his first impression of Latham. He should have done what long experience in handling men had told him to do; transfer him to another company or get him out of the Rangers entirely. He had thought he could handle Latham through patience and careful training. Now five men were dead.

Those who were left rode on, staring unseeingly ahead, each occupied with his own bitter summation of what had happened, each wondering what he could have done to bring at least one of those five out alive. They were unwilling to look at each other, vaguely ashamed that they had run but knowing that to have stayed would have been useless suicide. To have flung themselves from their horses, trying to fight off the attack from the scanty cover of the pass, would have been an empty gesture. The Indians would have pinned them down and they would have died within the rocky furnace, one by one. With bleak fury they raised their eyes to stare at Latham. The grin was wiped from his face now. He darted quick, furtive glances at the silent men, feeling their anger and condemnation. He licked at dry lips with an abrasive tongue and tried to summon the words and courage to speak, then decided against it. He was frightened by the implacable hatred he saw, feeling it close about him until he wanted to scream in terror.

Sul reined up where a small stream broke from underground to trickle between a stand of cottonwood. Without an order, the men dropped from their saddles and plodded wearily to the water, kneeling before it in almost devotional attitudes, drinking greedily. Then, one by one, they watered their mounts and led them away, their gaze upon Sul whose slitted eyes scanned the purpling sky.

Without words, the Rangers hunkered down in a half circle. Idly, they broke small twigs between their fingers while they watched Carter, dimly recognizing the silent rage that consumed him. Sul was a dedicated man. They had ridden with him long enough to know this. He held this isolated troop together through discipline tempered by wisdom and a sure knowledge of the country and its perils. Men followed him because he had their confidence.

There was in him a hatred for the lawless, a contempt for weakness which gained their respect.

Latham, pretending to be occupied with his saddle girth, flicked apprehensive eyes at the squatting men. He left his horse and with a pitiful effort at jauntiness made an attempt to join the silent men. No one moved to make room for him. He fidgeted and with trembling fingers tried to roll a cigarette. The paper tore, spilling out the fine, golden grains and the youth stared vacantly at the mangled remains.

"That was pretty good shooting back there, Latham." Sul's words cracked so unexpectedly that Latham jumped. "That was real good shooting."

The youth was puzzled. He stared at Carter and then managed a weak, hopeful smile. Maybe Carter was just going to yell at him, make him look like a fool in front of the others.

"It was comical the way that Indian fell." Sul continued in a monotone.

Some of Latham's confidence returned. He laughed but with little conviction. "Never knew what hit him." The boast was there.

"Yes, sir." Sul eyed him steadily. "It isn't every day you can kill an Indian and five Rangers with a single shot."

Suddenly Latham knew a paralyzing fear. This was a court of judgment. The silent, waiting men the jury. He watched with mounting terror as Sul took a rope from his saddle, hesitated and then quickly tossed it over the limb of a tree. Before he was aware of what was happening, two men had twisted his hands behind his back and lashed them there. It occurred so quickly that the scream of fear was late. Then he struggled in a frenzied panic, kicking out, yelling his impotent, hysterical, incredulous fear.

"What are you fixin' to do? What are you fixin' to do?" The question was repeated in a high, keening note that shrilled with desperation.

"I'm going to hang you, Latham!"

"You're crazy. Tell him he's crazy." Latham's glance implored the other men. "You ain't goin' to let a crazy man do a thing like this. How did I know it was goin' to turn out like it did? I figured a dead Indian was one less we had to worry about. How was I to know?"

"You knew because you had your orders. But you won't take orders. Because of you I lost five men. Five men who trusted me. Five men I knew and—and loved. Can you understand that? You're a murderer, Latham. You killed those men as sure as if you shot them down in the street. You're a senseless, idiotic killer, a mad dog loose." He nodded to the men who held the writhing prisoner. "Get it over with."

"You can't do this I tell you!" Latham screamed again as they dragged him toward his horse. "My—my old man'll kill you for this, Carter. He ain't goin' to let you hang me this way. He'll hunt you down. You know it. You can't let him do this." He screeched his alarm to the others, looking for some sign of compassion. Then his fear turned into helpless rage. "I know you're tough." He yelled accusingly at Carter. "You got a reputation. The hardest man in the Rangers but you ain't goin' to prove it on me." He twisted away from the imprisoning arms and threw himself to the ground, rolling over and over in the dirt in a frantic effort to escape.

They jerked him upright again and dragged him back. Froth appeared on his lips and broke into small bubbles. He was beyond speech now and a glazed film clouded the wild eyes.

The men watched impassively as Latham was thrown upon his saddle. The loop dropped over his head, jerked and snapped convulsively. Then it was over. Under the quick lash of a quirt, the riderless horse galloped past leaving a spinning form that seemed to bounce upon the air before it hung slack and limp, casting a lifeless shadow upon the ground.

While the sun coasted slowly down its great arc, Sul stood alone in the cottonwood grove. He was only half-aware of the twilight activity; the flights of the big, gray-white doves, which the Mexicans called *huilotas,* as they burst across the sky, the lazy circling of the hawks in

search of an evening meal, the small sounds of invisible
birds that knew the night as a friend. Behind Sul the men
waited and beyond them an elliptical mound of earth was
moistly dark.

He did not regret what he had done; there was no
question as to whether he had acted wisely or with a
rashness born of sudden anger. Latham had disobeyed
orders. He had caused the death of five men and jeop-
ardized every Ranger in the company. The full conse-
quences of the boy's action could not yet be measured. It
could easily send the Indians on a fury of sudden raids in
which men and women who had never heard the name of
Latham would be killed and tortured, their small farms
ravaged, their stock driven off. Justice, he told himself,
could not be diluted with mercy. It was as inflexible as the
laws of mathematics. Latham had killed five men. He had
been punished. That was the end of it. Even as he told
himself these things a small doubt nagged at him. Had he
failed in his duty? With more patience, a little additional
time, could he have taught Carey Latham a respect for
authority, an understanding of discipline, pride in his
office? He sighed wearily and turned away, walking
toward the silent men.

Chapter Two

The settlement of Davis stretched along a
twisted, ochre ribbon of rutted and pock-marked road. In
summer the ridges were baked to a flinty hardness. When
the rains came it was a stagnant river of almost impassable
mud. The buildings on both sides were a miscellaneous
collection of frame and adobe and a boardwalk provided a
footpath and a lounging place. Set starkly upon the plain,
it had no reason for existence save for the precious water
which lay only a few feet below the surface. Here the

wagon trains halted to fill their barrels and replenish their dwindling stocks from the general store. Cavalry detachments on their lonely patrols made it a frequent point of call. Through it, their eyes set upon some distant goal, passed the footloose, the straggling adventurers, the dispossessed from the southern states who had seen their world disappear at Appomattox. It was an orderly town, made so by the presence of the Rangers. Indistinguishable from a hundred other dusty settlements, it existed in a curious state of apathy, the people drained of animation by the daily monotony. Here the Anglos, the few Mexicans and a couple of dozen domesticated Indians lived with a quiet indifference to each other. Only on the monthly pay days did it liven up. Then the cowhands from distant spreads rode in to drink, gamble, argue and fight in the only saloon within fifty miles.

Dusty, bone-weary and tight-lipped, the Rangers rode down the street, scattering a mongrel assortment of sleeping dogs and foraging chickens. A few persons stood in the open doorways to watch them pass, counting, as they always did, the number of those who had ridden away against those who returned.

The headquarters of Company B, Texas Rangers, was set at the far end of the street. The building was a squared U of surprising grace. The weathered abode, hand smoothed, had a soft patina; the *portal,* a covered walkway built along the front and two sides, provided the only shade from the sun. In the single building were the mess hall, the barracks and the small room which Sullivan Carter used as an office.

Filing into the compound, the Rangers hit the ground with weary grunts and began to strip their horses. There was little talk and none of the rough horseplay which usually attended a return to the barracks. They heaved saddles and blanket rolls to the tack rail and led the dusty animals around to the back to water and feed. Sul, finishing his chore, looked down at the solemn-eyed Indian boy of ten or so who stood with silent hopefulness a few feet away. With a half-smile Sul nodded and the boy leaped to

the mount's bare back and proudly rode him out of sight
to the trough.

Legs spread to ease their stiffness, Sul looked across the
compound to where two heavy poles had been set deep
into the ground. Between them stretched a chain which
the Rangers ironically called "the trout line." Jails were
few and far between. The "hoosegows" were never meant
to house more than an occasional drunk who was tossed in
to sleep it off. The thieves, the rustlers, the "wanted men"
who were rounded up by the Rangers were shackled to the
trout line and kept prisoner there until an escort could be
spared to take them into Austin and the courts. Here, in
full view of the curious, they sat out the hot days and cold
nights, manacled to the chain which allowed them to stand
or sit but not to move beyond their place more than a few
inches.

There were four men on the line now. One stood,
soundlessly trying to attract Sul's attention. He grinned
sheepishly, shrugging his broad shoulders with an expression that indicated that his presence on the line was a
mystery to him. Sul studied him without recognition and
then scratched thoughtfully at his ear. He walked toward
the line and then moved along it, bending to lift a down-
tilted hat from a sullen, averted face or to study the
bleary, expressionless eyes that looked up at him without
recognition. He halted before the standing man with the
anxious, uncertain grin.

"What are you doing on the line, Cade?" Only in the
use of the name did Carter indicate that the man was
other than a stranger.

"Dogged ef I really know, Sul. An' that's a fact." There
was a clownish impudence in the reply. "It's all kind of a
mystery."

"Who are these men?" Sul indicated the others with a
jerk of his head.

"Drovers an' teamsters. Come in with a wagon train
yisteddy." The man called Cade waited.

"Drunk?"

"Well, not no more they ain't." A note of returning
confidence was in the voice.

"What about you?" Sul's eyes were granite.

"Not me no more, neither, Sul."

"All right. Tell me about it." There was no encouragement in the invitation.

"Well." Cade screwed up his features in an effort at concentration. "I was offen duty, down to the saloon. These fellas was a drinkin' some an' I had a few with 'em. Now, you know how likker sometimes gets to me. I don't always remember details so good. Anyhow," his shoulders jerked spasmodically, "a fracas started that was like to break up the place. First thing you know I had to lay 'em out, one by one, an drag 'em over here to the line for safe keepin'. Then," he looked hopefully at Sul for a sign of understanding, "I said to myself, 'Cade Kemper you're a drunk. You ain't fit to be a Ranger this minute. I'm goin' to chain you up with the others.' So, that's just what I did." He paused, trying to find a glimmer of understanding in Carter's cold eyes.

Sul grunted noncommittally, reaching into a hip pocket for a bunch of keys on a rawhide thong. He walked along the line, snapping open the padlocks, releasing the prisoners. For a moment they stamped their feet, rubbed at chafed wrists, stretched their backs and then, as a unit, shuffled on a diagonal path across the open stretch toward the saloon. As they neared the half-doors their pace accelerated. Looking after them Sul grinned to himself. Then, he pocketed the keys and turned away.

"Sul." The call was a mournful wail. "You ain't goin' to leave me here like this, are you?"

"You put yourself on the line. You ought to be able to get yourself off."

"But you don't understand, Sul." There was misery in the words. "It wasn't until after I'd snapped the lock that I remembered I'd left the keys in your office."

Carter masked a brief smile with the back of his hand. "I don't know why I bother with you, Cade." He shook his head.

"Because I'm a real good man in a pinch, Sul." Kemper's smile was ingenuous.

"I don't know about that." Sul opened the padlock.

"But you're the only man in the company who's idiot enough to lock himself up. Now, if I catch you taking a drink for the next sixty days you'll go back on the line and stay there."

"Yes, sir, Captain." A clumsy salute followed the words. "You know me. I'm off the stuff an' that's a fact."

Sul left him staring wistfully in the direction of the saloon. Crossing the compound he strode along the boarded *portal* and turned in at the doorway leading to the office.

It was a small room, bare of decoration except for a large map of Texas on the wall. On either side of it were the "Wanted" circulars sent out from Austin. In heavy black type were listed the descriptions of the men and their crimes. At a scarred table Pop Warner was bent over a sheet of paper. He wrote slowly, carefully, and paused to look up at Sul's entrance.

"I thought I'd better get to the report, Sul." He tapped the paper with a heavy finger.

Carter dropped wearily into a chair and nodded. Pop had voluntarily taken on the job of company clerk, preparing the reports which were sent at irregular intervals to Austin. He wrote in a beautiful script, shading his letters until the paper became almost a work of art.

"How do you want Latham entered?" The old man waited.

"Just the way it happened." Sul stretched his long legs, studying his boot tips.

"It would look better if we just listed him as a casualty, Sul."

"It's not supposed to look better." There was a sharp reprimand in the tone. "I hung him because he disobeyed orders and killed five men. That's reason enough for me."

"It might not be reason enough for Austin."

"Then let Austin come down and run the company." Carter stood up abruptly. "I had him executed. That's the way it was. That's the way it's going to read. I'm not covering up or making excuses." He went to the map, staring at it for a moment. At its side a piece of crayon was suspended on a string tacked to the wall. He picked it up and made a small circle to include the pass and within it wrote the numeral 5. All across the map were similar notations, marking the places where Rangers had died. Little mounds of earth, he thought, unmarked, unnoticed.

Aware that Pop was watching him, his expression grave, concerned and almost sympathetic, he turned from the map and walked to the open door, staring out across the dun-colored landscape. Its harshness was softened now by the brief twilight. What held him here? Many times he had asked himself that question, never finding an answer. It was a land of unpredictable dangers. In it men grew lean, tough and wary. Their homes were rude cabins or spartan barracks such as these. They were without social contacts or even the simplest comforts of life. Why did any of them stay? He shook his head. When you tried to find an explanation it just didn't make sense. The pay was a dollar a day and you provided your own horse and food. A man couldn't grow wealthy on that. Was it a deep passion for order? Why should these men who, not so long ago, had put aside their arms at the end of a bloody war between the states take them up again in defense of a land in which they had no roots, no ties? Perhaps the confusion of war had bred in them a yearning for stability. Was that why they chased rustlers, bandits and renegades until they came to accept danger and death as companions? Why did he, Sullivan Carter, one of a long line of Virginians whose family had produced doctors, lawyers and a few ministers, find himself on this scorched prairie, wearing the star of Texas, sworn to uphold its laws? What was Texas to him? He half-smiled. These were familiar questions. He honestly didn't know their answers. He felt no desire to police the world, to brandish authority. He started to turn away from the door when his eyes sharpened and he shaded them with both hands, peering at a faint dust cloud. After a few minutes the indistinct figures of mounted men emerged from the haze, stretching back in a dark, wavering line. He dropped his hands and grunted.

"We've had everything else today," he called over his shoulder, "now we've got soldiers."

Pop rose from the table and crossed to join him. Together they stood watching the approaching troop. The Rangers were inclined to be contemptuous of the military with its insistence that everything be done by the book. They were amused by its punctiliousness, its salutes and insistence upon rank. Grudgingly they conceded that perhaps the Army did a good job within the limitations drawn about it, but they didn't believe the task was better done by adding "Sir" to every word. It would have sent them into guffaws to have to call Sul, Sir. What the Army did with its spit and polish, its formations and parades, the Rangers, or so they held, did better, quicker.

Along the street, the sleeping dogs rose to greet the troops with a chorus of frantic barking. Men appeared from the stores, stables and saloon to watch the leisurely approach of the column. Even the smallest break in the daily monotony was welcomed as a diversion.

Sul turned away. "You'd better get a couple of extra places set. We'll probably have officers for supper." He grinned at Pop. "Then we'll find out how things should be done. I'd sure like to know. I've been trying to learn to call everything an 'incident' the way the Army does. It would come in real handy the next time we're ambushed or caught in a canyon like today. You take care of them, Pop, while I go and wash up."

Chapter Three

The young civilian riding beside an officer at the column's head turned eager, searching eyes from the landscape. Five days in the saddle had not dulled his interest in the novelty of this vast sea of mesquite, cactus and sage that rolled out to a seemingly limitless horizon. Texas! He savored the word, experiencing a tingle of excitement. Not only was he in Texas but a part of it. The Ranger's star pinned to his shirt was so new that it glinted brightly even in the fading light. The holstered revolver that was slung at the hip had never been fired. Yet, he already felt like a veteran. In his mind he had hunted rustlers, fought off Indian attacks and single-handedly brought the guilty and dangerous to justice.

"That Davis up ahead?" He nodded to where the low buildings were painted against the clear sky.

The officer smiled to himself at the barely concealed enthusiasm in the question, wishing that some of his re-cruits would bring the same quality along with their enlist-ment papers. He wondered, as he had so often, what the Rangers had to offer that brought such youths as this to their ranks. There was an undeniable aura of romance about the organization that the Rangers themselves perpet-uated. They were tough, seemingly fearless and dedicated men, relentless in their pursuit of the lawless; a breed of men who developed a similarity of speech, philosophy and, almost, a physical pattern. They walked and rode with a curious pride that the Army outposts had been unable to instill in their men.

"That's Davis, what there is of it." He answered the question now. "It's been a long ride. Tired?"

A grin of acknowledgement flashed across the boy's face. "Captain," the confession was wry. "I stopped being tired about three days ago. Now I'm just beat. I rode a lot back home, or that's what I thought, but it sure wasn't like this."

"The Rangers will toughen you." Captain John Macey studied his companion. "How old are you, Mr. Carter?"

"Twenty," Yancey Carter replied promptly. "Well, nineteen, really, but I'll be twenty in a few months."

"You're almost an old man for the Rangers, then." Macey chuckled dryly. "It seems to me that they take their recruits out of swaddling cloths and that they're born with a gun in one hand and a bottle in the other. Aside from your brother, what brought you to Texas?"

"I guess it was Sul's being here, mostly. He's about the only kin I have left. Oh, there are a few cousins scattered around Virginia and South Carolina but I never counted them as real kin. There wasn't much left back home by the time you Yankees . . ." He halted abruptly.

"Yankees. Rebs," Macey spoke understandingly. "They're only words now. At least I'd like to think so."

"Anyhow," Yancey continued without embarrassment, "you Yankees sure raised hell in Virginia. Our place near Petersboro was burned. The Negrahs all took off, yellin' 'emancipation' like it was some magic word that would clothe and feed them from now on without working. They came drifting back later, moving into the cabins, waiting for someone to tell them what to do. I still can't figure what you Yankees expected to accomplish by turning them loose without seeing that there was someone around to take care of them. Freedom! They don't know what it means or what to do with it. Anyhow, I sure didn't know how to handle them and I didn't feel like going back to the University. So, I headed West and here I am."

"Does your brother know you're coming?"

The short laugh carried with it honest amusement. "Sul? Uh-uh! I guess Sul thinks I'm still in short pants. He'd want to cut a switch and chase me back to school. An older brother, sometimes, never lets you grow up. We haven't seen each other for five years and he never was one for writing much. I just don't know what he's like any more."

"You'll find him changed, I expect." Macey spoke reflectively. "Captain Carter and I don't always see eye to eye on things. It isn't anything personal, you understand. He gets impatient with the Army, I expect, and is used to doing things his way which," he laughed softly, "isn't at all by the book. But, he has his job to do and I have mine. We try to stay out of each other's way. He has the reputation of being a very tough man, Mr. Carter; tough and hard to handle."

"Sul was always sort of ramrod-stiff." Yancey nodded understandingly. "Not mean or hard to get along with but just correct. I guess that's the word for it. Correct. He couldn't stand anyone slacking off. When he did something it was finished off right down to the end. There were never any loose strings to be tied after Sul got through."

He smiled to himself. "A brother like that can get to be quite a trial after awhile."

The first of the settlement's dogs reached the column. They raced around, generating their excitement, nipping at the horses. The animals danced nervously and then, scenting water and feed, quickened their pace voluntarily until the troops were moving at a trot. Yancey winced at the shock of hooves meeting hard earth. Then he drew himself up with an effort. He wasn't going to ride up to Sul slumped in the saddle. His eyes swept the buildings. This was Davis, a Ranger post, and he was a Ranger.

At the command, the troops drew up in dismissal formation within the compound. Yancey dropped from his horse and led it to a hitching rail. A couple of men, lounging against the building's side eyed him with curiosity.

"Where'll I find Captain Carter?" He tied the horse.

They stared at him silently, appraisingly, their glances not missing the star worn so openly. "I guess you'll find him out to the back—Ranger." The title was added almost derisively although the face was without any particular expression.

For a second, Yancey experienced a flare of temper. What was so funny about a new Ranger? None of them had been born in the service. They had all started new and had had to learn.

"My name's Carter." He put out his hand which, after a moment, the Rangers took solemnly.

"Any kin to Sul?"

"Brother." Yancey dropped the single word, aware that they were studying him with new interest.

"Walk through there." A jerk of a head indicated a covered passageway separating the buildings. "Likely enough you'll find him."

Yancey nodded and moved toward the walkway, his boots sounding unnaturally loud on the boards. He had hoped that Sul would be there to watch him ride up so he could see the bewilderment on his brother's face. He had rehearsed the meeting many times. It would be casual,

easy; the way a Ranger would take things, without a show
of excitement or emotion.

Several men were spaced along a watering trough behind the barracks. They splashed and snorted as they
washed. Army issue suspenders dangling about their
knees, the clay-gray tops of woolen underwear unbut-
toned, revealing startlingly white skin where the deep tan
ended at the throat. An Indian girl, clad in a shapeless
skirt, a papoose in a sling upon her young back, stood a
few yards away. Her brooding eyes were fixed upon a
young Ranger, watching as he finished washing and ran
wet hands through his long hair. An older man glanced at
her and nudged his companion. Together, with hoarse
croakings they began to sing.

> "We've traveled this wide world over,
>   But this we're tellin' you,
>   We never seed no papoose before
>   With eyes o' Chiny blue!"

A roar of delighted laughter swept over the men at the
trough and the two minstrels whacked each other on the
back, doubled up with mirth. Solemnly, the Indian girl
turned and walked away while the young Ranger looked
after her in silent misery.

"Why don't you boys knock it off and let Harper
alone?" Sul, at the far end of the trough, bent to shave
before a broken triangle of mirror, fingered the now
smooth curve of his jawline. For a moment his eyes rested
on Yancey without recognition. He turned again to the
glass and then suddenly snapped upright, incredulous and
surprised. "Yancey!" He shouted the name, unbelievingly.

"How're you, Sul?" The younger brother moved forward, sauntering with a contrived casualness until they
faced each other. Concealing an elated grin, he snapped a
crisp salute. "Ranger Yancey Carter reporting, Sir!"

Open-mouthed, the other Rangers regarded the salute,
turning questioningly to each other at this display of

formality. Sul continued to stare at his brother, then a small flicker of amusement lighted his eyes.

"This isn't VMI," he said deliberately. "We don't go in much for saluting around here." Carefully, he laid the razor down and stepped forward, his hands gripping Yancey's shoulders. "Say that over again, will you?"

"What?" Yancey was enjoying his brother's mystification.

"That part about Ranger Yancey Carter." The hands tightened irritably.

"I signed up in Austin. I've got a paper to prove it." He made a gesture toward his shirt pocket.

Sul shook his head. "I believe you. I don't want to see it. No one would be fool enough to come to this place unless he had signed up."

"Aren't you glad to see me?" The excitement of the long-anticipated meeting flickered out. Yancey searched his brother's face for some indication of warmth.

"No." The word was cold, decisive. "I mean I'm not glad to see you here. Didn't they know in Austin you were my brother?"

"Sure they did. I told them. I asked to be assigned to your company."

"And they sent you?" Sul shook his head. "Someone ought to know better than that. Someone sure ought to know a whole hell of a lot better than that." He looked around, aware that the men had stopped their washing and were watching and listening intently. "This is my kid brother, Yancey." He made the introduction abruptly.

A ragged chorus of "Howdy" followed, the men shuffling forward awkwardly to shake Yancey's hand, their eyes traveling between the two brothers. Then they drifted away leaving them alone.

"That kid stuff is all over, Sul." Quick temper flared in the words. "I don't want to start out here being anyone's kid brother. I'm a man grown."

"Are you?" The question was flat, toneless. Deliberately, he bent again to the mirror and set the blade against . his cheek. The rasp of steel on bristles was an angry sound. Twisting his mouth to reach the corner of an upper lip, Sul paused.

"You know what this is going to do; having you here, I mean?"

"It means you have another Ranger. That's what it means." Yancey was defiant.

"It means I have a brother. It means that every dirty job that comes along will have you on it. You'll go up against men who can put half a dozen slugs in your belly before you can get that new gun out of the leather. You'll ride after cattle thieves who know a thousand tricks of the country and who will bushwhack you in the middle of a thousand miles of prairie while you're admiring the scenery. You'll trail Indians you can't see or hear until it's too late. That's what it means." He paused, the impatience giving way to a plea for understanding. "I could take a new man and teach him, look after him until he learned enough to take care of himself. But, you're my brother. Every man in the company will be watching to see if I give it to you the easy way."

"I don't want any favors." Yancey's eyes reflected his brother's stubbornness.

"Favors!" Sul snorted the word. "Boy, don't you understand what I'm saying? I'm trying to tell you that you'll have it rougher than any man in the company because your name is Carter." He turned again to the mirror and finished shaving with short, swift strokes. Then he rinsed his face, stropped the blade and put it away in a case. "Let's eat," he said abruptly. "We can talk about it later." He started to turn away, hesitated and swung about with a half-apologetic smile, offering his hand. "What I said doesn't mean I'm not glad to see you. I am. You look fine. That's the way I want to keep you looking. We're about the last of the family. One of us has to stay alive."

Yancey met the pressure of his brother's hand gratefully. Secretly he had always been a little overwhelmed by Sul. "I figure on staying alive. Every Ranger in Texas had to learn. That includes even you." He grinned. "I don't guess you were born omniscient, Sul, no matter what you may think about it."

Sul's eyes lighted, then he chuckled softly. "I don't think I've heard a word like that since I've been in Texas." He dropped an arm about Yancey's shoulder and then withdrew it self-consciously. "Come on. I'm hungry."

Chapter Four

They sat at long, bare tables in the low-beamed mess hall. There was no talk, only the sounds of men eating with a ravenous hunger. They wolfed down the chunks of tough, freshly-slaughtered beef stewed with chilies and tomatoes, sopping up the gravy with the fragrant tortillas made from meal, hand-ground in stone metates by the Indian women. They grunted requests for a steaming casuela of frijoles and belched their appreciation of the strong, black coffee which was carried in soot-smudged pots by a ragged Mexican boy. As they finished, they left the table without a word and drifted outside to smoke. Finally only Sul, Captain Macey and Yancey were left at the table.

The Army officer took a worn leather case from his blouse and offered the twisted cheroots it held to his host. "They're not Havana, Captain," he apologized, "but they are tobacco, of sorts."

Yancey shook his head but Sul selected one and sniffed it. "It seems to me," he spoke thoughtfully, "the least Cuba could do would be to send us some good cigars for all the stolen Texas cattle it's getting."

"Cuba?" Yancey leaned forward on the table, anxious to pick up any information he could. "Do cattle thieves take beef all the way to Cuba?"

"They take it across the Rio Grande into Mexico." Sul lit his cheroot. "We've got a border river that, in some places, you could spit across but it might as well be the

Pacific Ocean. The rustlers drive the stolen cattle across and thumb their noses at us. We can't chase them and they know it. Then they ship the steers, a boatload a week, I hear, to Cuba. It isn't even a half-kept secret that General Cortina has a standing order for a boatload of cattle every seven days. It's a big operation. There is someone on this side with a ranch, probably somewhere down in the Big Bend country, who uses his place as a gathering point. From there they make a drive across the Rio Grande and Cortina's vaqueros take over." He scratched a wavering line on the table boards. "For, maybe, a hundred and fifty miles on this side of the river Americans have abandoned their crops and herds, given up trying to settle there. They are afraid to travel except in armed parties. In the small towns the judges and sheriffs don't even attempt to execute or enforce the law outside of the towns unless they can get troops to protect them. Bandits from Mexico cross over to murder and steal, raiding the unprotected towns and then race back to Reynosa, Matamoros and laugh when we draw up at the border. It stinks!" He glared at Captain Macey as though to place the blame on him.

"I know." The Army officer nodded sympathetically. "Everything you say is true, Captain. But our hands are tied. We can't invade Mexico and violate the sovereignty of a country. Washington won't let us. You know that."

"Washington had better let someone do something or Texas, along the border, will be bled bone-white." Sul stabbed the knife's point into the table. "We've got Indians here!" He withdrew the blade and with a gesture of exasperation pricked at another spot. "Border bandits, road agents here. Yankee scum there." He hesitated and a shadow of a smile touched his mouth. "All right, Captain. Southern scum also, maybe. I guess we're not all congenitally noble just because we were born south of the Mason-Dixon. Anyhow, I'm right in the middle of ten thousand square miles with a company of thirty men. How am I supposed to keep the peace in an area like that?" He glared at the unoffending Macey. "I sure don't get any help from you."

The Army officer was undisturbed. "Do you suggest we declare war on Mexico to help you put down the cattle thieving?" The question had a mild bite.

"I don't know," Carter said wearily. "I have the Provisional Governor on my back and he's carrying the complaint of every rancher that's lost a yearling. Maybe the Navy could step in, patrol outside the gulf ports and halt every cattle boat that puts out. I know this stolen beef is going to Havana. We put a man in Brownsville and another in Bagdad. They counted sixteen different brands on the steers being loaded. The ranchers who owned the brands swore that they had never sold the cattle." He spat his disgust. "They don't even bother to burn the brands off any longer." He stood up abruptly. "I can't go into Mexico with any force but I'll tell you what I can do. I'm going to comb through the Big Bend until I find the ranch they are using as a collection depot on this side. It has to be a big spread, bigger than any we know about. If I can locate that, then maybe we can break up the drives before they get started."

Macey rose and Yancey left his seat to stand with them. He had been intently fascinated by this unfolding of a broad picture of lawlessness. This was all a vital part of the legend as it had been told and retold.

"I'll tell you something you may not know, Captain." Macey blew softly on the tip of his cheroot. "Your old friend, Iron Shirt, is doing a lot of maneuvering under cover these days. He's holding councils with the Sioux, the Apache, the Comanches, Kiowas and Lipans. They are making big talk about something. It may be a general uprising."

"Who is Iron Shirt?" Yancey glanced with bright interest at Sul.

"A Mescalero chief." Carter replied almost absently. He was assaying what Macey had just said, weighing the possibility of fresh Indian trouble on a large scale. Then he shook his head. "They'd need more guns, powder and bullet metal than they can lay their hands on."

"If they are stealing the cattle it could be for the

purpose of a trade with Cortina. Beef in exchange for the guns and what goes with them." Macey suggested.

"It could be." Sul grinned. "An Indian uprising is the Army's business, Captain."

"It would be the business of every man, woman and child in Texas. You know that." Macey moved with them toward the door.

Outside they stood for a minute. The night was a black shroud, wrapping the land in silence. A faint breeze brought with it the fresh, sweet smell of sun-scorched earth as it yielded the day's heat. Save for the saloon, there were no lights on the main street.

"Well," Macey held out his hand. "Thanks for your hospitality, Captain. We'll be on our way at daybreak. Good luck to you, Ranger." He smiled at Yancey and left them with a short, formal bow.

Sul's eyes followed the erect figure until it disappeared. Then he sighed—a short, troubled sound. "Let's take a walk, Yancey."

"Iron Shirt is an unusual name for an Indian, isn't it?" Yancey matched his brother's stride.

"He's a pretty unusual Indian." Sul chuckled. "A Mescalero chief and a man with a lot of ambition. He thinks he can lick the United States if he can just get enough guns together." He laughed again, softly and with honest amusement. "The son-of-a-gun has half the Indians believing that he can't be killed. Somewhere he got hold of an old Spanish breastplate. A cuirass, I think they call it. He wears it under his buckskin and used to make a great show of letting the bucks shoot at him. With the old, smooth bore muskets they had, the bullets just bounced off of him. That sort of thing makes big medicine among the braves. They would follow him anywhere."

In the lonely distance, a coyote raised a quavering, melancholy wail followed by fierce, rapid yapping. Then the night again retreated into silence.

They halted atop a slight rise. Behind them only a couple of lights showed in the windows of the Ranger headquarters. Yancey looked up at the sky, brilliant with its spangled ornamentation.

"You're going back home, Yancey." Sul spoke abruptly. "I've been thinking it over. I'll fix your enlistment with Austin. I don't want you here."

The younger man's features tightened stubbornly and in that moment he was a startling replica of his brother. "I don't figure it's up to you, Sul." He kept the tone moderate with an effort. "I signed for a job and I'll do it. There are things I'll have to learn. Stop thinking you have to get in on my fights the way you did when we were kids. I'm a man and I'll pull a man's weight."

"You're a boy!" The challenge was short. "You haven't any idea what you're talking about. This isn't spit and polish with formation every afternoon on a parade ground. You belong back in school. Go home, make something of yourself. Folks always said you would. How old are you, anyhow?"

"I'm almost twenty. You know that."

Sul grasped his brother's shoulders and wheeled him about. "Then let me tell you something. Out here, with the Rangers, if you're real lucky you may live to be twenty-one. That isn't near long enough, boy, believe me it isn't."

"How old were you when you came to Texas, Sul?" The question was mild.

"That's got nothing to do with it. Things were different for me. I got old in the war. You're still a boy. You've got an idea that this is a romantic business. That you'll go off, rootin'-tootin' to chase bandits, hunt down marauding Indians or take a thief into custody like it was just a masquerade party back in Virginia. No one gets hurt. Everyone just says good night and goes home."

"Why do you stay?" Yancey asked reasonably. "Am I supposed to believe you were born to be a Ranger in Texas? You were going to study medicine and take over father's practice when the war was over. What happened? Why did you change your mind?"

Sul's frown deepened for a second and then he shook his head. "I don't know. I came to Texas. I ran away, I guess, from what I didn't want to face. Everything as I had known it was gone. I couldn't sit on a rubble heap."

"You could have helped clear it away. A lot of men

came back from the war and did just that. Someone had
to."

Sul nodded. The guilt was there and he had to admit it.
"I guess," he spoke softly, "I just don't like the feeling of
being licked."

"You know what they say back home?" Yancey's laugh
was quietly amused. "They say the Yankees didn't win the
war. The South only lost it." He paused. "But, let's get
this straight. I'm here. I'm a Ranger and I'm going to
stay. It would be better if you liked it, easier for us both.
Like it or not, I'm staying."

"All right." Sul kept from shouting with an effort.
"Stay." He thrust an accusing finger against his brother's
chest. "But let me tell you something. You're going to be a
lonely man. You'll eat and sleep with your guns. That star
they pinned on you at Austin isn't only a badge. It's a
target. You're going to learn that a coyote's howl probably
isn't a coyote at all but one Indian talking to another,
dividing up your hair. You'll find out that every time you
ride into a town, push through the doors of a saloon or
spend a night on the prairie there'll be a fast gun waiting
for a chance to make a name for himself by killing a
Ranger. You're the law, and not many persons in Texas
care much for the law. They'd rather settle things among
themselves. So don't look for gratitude or friends. You're
not going to find them."

"You're not scaring me, Sul." Yancey seemed amused
by his brother's vehemence.

"You'd better get scared." Sul turned away with a
disgusted snort. "If you get scared now you may live to be
twenty-one. I want to tell you that's almost senile in the
Rangers."

They covered the distance to the barracks without further words and then halted outside a window within a
narrow oblong of light.

"You'd better get a good night's sleep." Sul was abrupt.
"We're going to make a sweep tomorrow, down into the
Big Bend. It's tough country, probably the roughest
you've ever seen. Sometimes you'll think you're in a forgotten corner of Hell. I don't know how long we'll be

gone. I'm going to try and find something. If I do, we may have to fight our way in and out again." His tone softened. "I'll spot you with Pop and Manning. They're old hands, about as old as you get in this business. Stick with them and take their advice."

"I thought you said no favors, no special treatment?" The reminder was mocking.

"That's no favor. Pop and Manning don't have to look for trouble. It comes right up and spits in their eyes most of the time."

The shower of adobe and the splintering crack of a rifle's report seemed to sound simultaneously. Instinctively Sul hit the ground, one shoulder sweeping to knock Yancey's feet from under him. He heard the boy's surprised and painful grunt as he slammed into the dirt. Flattening himself and holding down his brother's shoulder, Sul peered into the darkness. A tongue of fire licked wickedly at the night; they heard the report again, felt the crumbling mud from the wall sprinkle coarse powder upon them.

"Sul! Sul Carter!" The voice of the unknown assailant was as brittle as the breaking of glass. "This is Rale Latham, Carter. You know why I'm here. You killed my boy; hung him like a common horse thief. Everyone in Davis knows about it. You hear me, Carter?"

"I hear you." Sul's reply was without anger, wearily resigned. "Put that rifle away, Rale. You're not going to shoot me."

"That's where you're wrong, Carter. You're a dead man this minute, only you don't know it."

The rifle's flash was a wavering, crimson point. Men who had tumbled from the barracks, crowding doorways and windows, ducked from the exposed spots for cover as a slug buried itself in the adobe. Desperately seeking to make himself invisible, Yancey found a moment to marvel at what was happening. Out there, somewhere, a man was intent upon killing Sul. He, Yancey Carter, who had never seen a gun fired in anger, was lying with his face buried in Texas dirt while a man he had never heard of shot at him.

"Are you on your belly, Sul?" The laugh was dry, crackling, as maniacal as the sound of a loon in the marsh. "I'd like to see that. Crawl some for me, Sul."

"Don't be a fool, Rale." The indignity of his position left Sul in helpless anger. "If you know what I did then you know why I did it." Mentally he cursed the man who had spread the story for a loose-mouthed idiot.

"You murdered my boy, Carter."

Yancey would have sworn that the man was weeping somewhere out there in the dark. "What's he talking about, Sul?" he whispered.

Sul shook his head without replying; his head raised furtively and his eyes swung over the night.

"I'm going to kill you, Carter. You know that."

"Shoot then and be damned." Sul yelled the invitation. His gun was out and he waited for the flash that would give him a momentary target.

"Not tonight, Carter." The declaration was triumphant. "I could have picked you off there by the window if I'd wanted to. You know that. I want you to know how it feels to live with it for a while. I want you to walk and ride and sleep with it; to jump and look over your shoulder every time you hear a noise." A long silence followed, as though Latham was waiting for a reply. Then they heard a horse's angry snort as spurs were dug into its side and the muffled thud of hooves as Latham galloped away.

Cautiously, Sul pulled himself up and stood, brushing the dirt from his shirt. His eyes followed the rider as men poured out of the barracks.

"Do you want him, Sul?" Parker Manning was at their side.

"No!" The word was clipped. Sul turned to Yancey and then dug at the corners of his mouth with a fist to hide a grin. "Still want to stick around?"

"He was shooting at you, not me." Yancey was almost too casual. "I didn't hear him say anything about Yancey Carter."

"He'll take you if he can't get me. Remember that and the name, Rale Latham."

Chapter Five

Within the great arc of the river, as it spills its way to the Gulf of Mexico, lies the country of the Big Bend. It is a region of jagged mountains, lush valleys and of silences so deep that it seems the world ended here.

They had been traveling for five days, combing this forbidding region without finding what Sul was certain must be there. Now and then they had come upon a miserable collection of adobe huts around which a few scrawny chickens scratched disconsolately in search of food. Skeletal dogs raised a fearsome clamor at their approach and then, bony tails between their legs, slunk away, a weak snarl trailing in their throats. It was a forgotten, primitive section of the State, where the people lived almost as had their cave-dwelling ancestors centuries ago. The multi-colored cliffs scaled abruptly to the sky and the trees were twisted into tortured and grotesque shapes. Now and then the Rangers had come upon a lonely goat herd or a boy tending a few sheep. Occasionally, they found a small settlement of rude huts, an effort at communal life; but for the most part it was a deep well of silence, forbidding and awesome.

The men and women in the settlements were a mixture of Apache and Mexican and their dialect was an almost incomprehensible blending of Spanish and Indian tongue. They stared at the Rangers through lusterless eyes, stood in silence until they passed. Sul sometimes squatted with the men in an effort at consultation. They spoke grudgingly and the conversation was carried on with a few words and signs. To the questions put to them, they only shook their heads. They knew of no large ranch concealed within the mountain valleys. They were poor people who raised their small patches of beans and maize, tended their goats.

What, their expressions seemed to ask, had they to do with ranches or Rangers? When Sul indicated a couple of hides stretched on the drying frames with the brands of two different ranches clearly visible, his pointed questioning was met by an indifferent shrug. The cattle had been found dead of some mysterious illness. Was a man to leave them where they fell? Since they were already dead, what harm was there in skinning them and tanning the hides?

Listening, understanding nothing but an occasional word in Spanish, Yancey could feel the resentment at the intrusion. There was a bitterness that seemed to ask: What business have you here? Once in a while, he imagined that the Indians were laughing at them behind a deliberate conspiracy of feigned ignorance; that their stupidity was contrived. Sul was patient, although Yancey now and then detected a quick harshness, a tightening of the jaw, a sudden coldness in the gray eyes that revealed a disciplined anger as his interrogation was met with a doltish grin, a vacant shake of the head or a quick exchange of sly glances.

Save for these occasional halts, they encountered no human within the almost impassable reaches of the Big Bend. Wild life, though, seemed to swarm about them. The small, Mexican mule or black-tailed deer stood to watch their passage with limpid-eyed curiosity. Bands of snorting wild hogs, called *javelinas* by the men, went hurtling through the underbrush with idiotic intensity. At night, the silence was rent by the scream of a bobcat or the odd, coughing sound of a mountain lion. On the sheer cliffs, they sometimes caught a glimpse of the Texas bighorn, mountain sheep, balanced majestically against the sky. One night Park Manning had rolled with a frantic curse from his blanket to stamp to death a four-foot rattlesnake that had crept to his side for warmth. He cut the buttoned, rasping tail from the writhing carcass and put it into his shirt pocket, amusing himself at odd moments by trying out variations of its deadly whirr by trembling it between his fingers.

Although he had scant knowledge of the country,

Yancey realized that they could search here for months without finding the ranch Sul was hunting. If they came across it, the discovery would be by accident. They rode into blind passes from which there was no exit and retraced the weary miles. They made trail to the tops of ragged plateaus from which they could look down into the hidden valleys while Sul swept a glass across the horizon. They made camp at night in rocky pockets, partly shielded by the cliffs, and slept with their guns in their hands while two Rangers stood guard and a third kept watch over the hobbled horses. In such a thinly populated country, Yancey thought this over-cautious. Riding with Pop, he put the question to the older man.

"What are we afraid of?"

Pop turned this over in his mind gravely. "I wouldn't say anyone is exactly scared, boy." He studied Yancey with a faint smile. "Cautious, maybe. This is hostile country."

Yancey laughed. "The Indians I've seen didn't look as though they had ambition enough to kill a rabbit for stew, let alone jump fifteen armed men. What would they fight us with?"

"Bows and arrows, clubs, stones and slings. They've been killing each other that way for a thousand years or more. There's no reason to suspect it wouldn't work on us. An Indian will take almost any risk to get hold of a rifle, your knife, some ammunition, a horse. Give them the opportunity and they'd jump us, swarming out from a hundred hiding places. Don't get the idea we're not being watched. They know every move we've made since we entered here. Besides a natural cupidity there's a lot of just plain meanness that's been festering in them for a long time. They're a mongrel breed. Spanish soldiers up from Mexico dropped out of ranks and disappeared. They mated with Indian girls, Apaches, Lipans. Desperadoes, renegades, deserters from the Army have vanished in the Big Bend and left their untamed blood to mingle with those who were already here. Now, they are inbred, suspicious, resentful and cunning. No one has any idea what

the scattered population would total." He chuckled. "I'd
sure hate to try and take a census."

"How long will Sul stay down here?" Yancey was
saddle-weary and the novelty of the expedition which in
the beginning had had some of the same appeal for him as
the hunting trips he and Sul used to take in Virginia, was
wearing thin.

"I guess you don't know your brother very well, do
you?" Pop offered him a twist of chewing tobacco which
Yancey refused. "He'll sweep this country until he's satisfied. That could be weeks or months. He doesn't think
much about time when he's on a hunt for someone or
something. You'll get callused in the right place and then
it won't seem so bad."

At the end of the second week, traveling south by east,
they came to the juncture of the Pecos and Rio Grande.
Here the current was fast as the river rushed down past
Del Rio and Eagle Pass toward Laredo on its way to
distant Brownsville and the Gulf. Beside the river the men
waited without comment for Sul to make up his mind. A
few spoke wistfully to each other of the cantinas and girls
of Brownsville or Matamoros but they made no effort to
intrude this wishful thinking upon Carter. They had ridden with him too long, knew him too well. He was as tired
as they were, but if he said they would go back into the
mountains they would accept the decision without a word.
Discipline had become a part of their character. Of all the
men, Sul Carter was the best fitted to lead them and they
took his estimate of a situation without question.

Try as he might, Yancey could not get close to Sul. On
this hunt the man seemed continually preoccupied. At
night, around the fire, he sat with the others, staring into
the flames. He was one of them but at the same time
alone. When he spoke to Yancey his tone and manner
were no different than he used in talking with the men. He
was neither curt nor friendly. It was an almost splendid
detachment. He was decisive but not curt, demanding but
never overbearing. Although he missed the once-shared
warmth that had existed between the brothers, Yancey
was grateful that he had been permitted to take his place

with the Rangers as an untried recruit without any privilege because of kinship. It had been a hard, bone-jolting trip and no one knew this better than the men who rode with him. Feeling the weariness of their own bodies they knew how much more untrained muscles would have suffered. They made no comment, asked no questions, offered no advice, but Yancey could sense their approval, their acceptance. He was being tried and toughened, hammered by this expedition into the mold that would eventually cast him as a Ranger.

Stretched out on the ground now, allowing the earth's heat to creep assuasively through weary bodies, they lay near the river's high bank, listening to the purling water, idly following with their eyes the soaring climb of the ever-present buzzards. They waited while Sul squatted nearby and made aimless tracings in the dirt with a stick. Finally he grunted, tossed the twig away and stood up.

"I think we'll ride on down towards Mier and into Brownsville. Chet has been there for a month now. We'll find out what he has to say." One of the rare smiles illuminated his face briefly. "I figure we might make an overnight stop at Don Porfirio's." He jerked his head in the direction of the river. "It might be a good idea for you all to use some of that water to wash away the stink. I don't want Don Porfirio to think I've brought him a litter of polecats as guests."

With delighted whoops, the men began shucking their travel-stained clothes. Brownsville offered a variety of cosmopolitan delights. There would be hotel beds to sleep in, bars to lean against, whiskey to be drunk and girls to be dandled. Shouting their plans to each other, they skidded down the slope and into the river, sluicing themselves in the running current, wallowing in deep pools with contented snorts. Listening to their yells, watching as they mauled and ducked each other, Yancey laughed to himself. This is the way kids would behave at a swimming hole. He listened to their noisy speculations about Brownsville and their hopeful talk for a real fandango with the servant girls at Don Porfirio's.

"Don Porfirio?" Park Manning mused over Yancey's

question while rubbing himself vigorously with a handful of sand in place of soap. "A real, Spanish grandee, I guess you could call him. Don Porfirio Ramos y Mendoza. He settled here in Texas a long time ago when it was part of Mexico. I guess he's an American now but everyone still calls him Don Porfirio. He had a land grant from the King of Spain that stretched maybe fifty miles back of the river. He still runs the biggest spread in these parts. It's all open range so no one worries much about boundaries except where water is concerned. A man can usually work over as much land as he can hold. He and Sul are old friends. You'll see quite a place."

Chapter Six

The black smoke was an ugly stain against the afternoon sky. From a low ridge, the Rangers gazed at it and then spurs were kicked and the company bounded forward, strung out in a single line. Although each of the men knew there was no need for haste, that those who once lived on the small ranch crouched within the broad valley were beyond help now, their anger drove them to a headlong gallop. They did not look at each other but stared over the thrusting heads of their mounts. Their eyes had suddenly grown cold.

The spectacle before them was a familiar one. A few charred buildings, the empty corral, the evidence of senseless, Indian savagery that struck and disappeared. Always it left them with the helpless feeling of impotence. There just weren't enough men in Texas to cover and protect it all and these small, isolated ranches were falling one by one.

A few wisps of flame still licked about the piles of blackened rubble. A dog, disembowled, lay flattened against the grassless earth. Just beyond the smoking mound that had been the main house, the heat-seared bodies of a man, a woman and a young boy were sprawled. The green flies rose in a frantic swarm from the bloodied heads as the Rangers approached.

The men moved in a semicircle and stared with inarticulate fury. Sul turned to Yancey and pushed him lightly on the shoulder.

"I want you to take a good look." The voice was almost weary. "You're going to see it a lot of times."

Yancey felt the sickness curdling in his throat at the sight and the sweet, heavy odor of singed flesh and dried blood. He turned away, wanting to retch.

Watching the boy, Pop spoke quietly to Sul. "You're being pretty rough, aren't you? Giving it to him in big pieces."

"Does it come in small pieces?" Sul jerked his eyes away from the figure of his brother. He shook his head. "Let's dig some holes for them. That's about all we can do."

They buried what was left of John Barstow and his family and the late afternoon breeze, winnowing over the plains, brushed across the newly-turned graves. They did their work quickly and without comment. It was a task performed many times in many places. Although they would not have expressed it, they felt the lonely uneasiness of men who try to fight what they cannot see and when they left the place each man sought the company of another. They rode close together in silent communion.

Instinctively, Pop Warner had guided his horse until he was beside Yancey. The boy stared straight ahead. He was still queasy over what he had seen and ashamed over the weakness that had caused him to vomit uncontrollably before the others.

"Feeling better?" Pop did not look at him.

"I'm all right." Yancey's reply was stiff.

"You don't have to be ashamed. It isn't something you ever really get used to."

Yancey half-turned in the saddle to confront the man. "Aren't we going to do anything about it? Three people murdered and Sul just riding off this way."

"What do you want to chase, boy? If you were Sul what would you do?" The questions were patient, sympathetic.

"I—I'd sure be looking for the Indians who did it." The statement carried no conviction.

Pop bit into a twist of tobacco. "Where, Yancey? Where would you look?" His hand swept out to cover the vast, empty space of the plains. "Whoever killed Barstow and his family, ran off his few cattle and stock. They broke up into small parties and took different directions. You could hunt for years and never find them."

"But we're the law. That ought to mean something; an obligation, maybe. Without it the whole state turns into nothing but a pack of wild animals at each others' throats."

Pop nodded. "We're the law. We're all there is in a country where you could set down and lose half a dozen eastern states."

"Then we ought to have more men. Doesn't Texas realize that?"

"When you think about it, Yancey, there isn't any real inducement for a man to join. They're offered a dollar a day and a short life. Oh, we get them, young like you or old like me, but mostly they don't last long. After awhile you get the feeling that Texas is being built on the shoulders of dead Rangers."

Chapter Seven

The *estancia* of Don Porfirio lay beneath a quarter moon. The thick, adobe walls of the main house gave it the appearance of a fortress, grim and unyielding. Within the great patio, about which the house was built, there was music, laughter and the flaming illumination of pitch-filled torches. Along the top of the walls, candles in oiled paper sacks weighted with sand lifted small points of yellow light which danced in the night's breeze.

The musicians, by day, were Don Porfirio's vaqueros; lean, hard-riding men who had been born and reared on the ranch without ever leaving its acres. Now, for this fiesta in honor of Dona Marguerita's saint's day, they were dressed in the glittering costume of the charro with spangled and silver ornamentation that reflected the light with prismatic brilliance. Their instruments were traditional; three guitars, a violin and a single cornet. To the rhythm of the strings, the horn added the curious, wailing note of the flamenco; the wild, gypsy music of a Spain they had never known. The men and girls of the ranch danced with laughing abandon or, as the tunes changed, with a stately classicism. Drawn up in a solid group at one side of the patio were the Rangers who had not yet summoned the courage to take a partner.

Within the shadowy portal that extended along three sides of the patio, Don Porfirio and his guests watched the dancers. House servants, men in the white *calzones* of the Mexican peon, moved to refill glasses or offer trays of food.

Don Porfirio was a tall, handsome man in his early fifties, spare and almost ascetic in appearance but with the lean hardness of a soldier. He smiled contentedly to himself and kept time to the music with a light tapping of his fingers on the wicker arm rest of his chair. Seated next to him was his wife, Marguerita, some twenty years younger, with the fresh, olive complexion and flashing eyes of a girl. Dona Marguerita had never admitted to an isolation in this new and alien land to which she had been brought as a bride. For her there was no world beyond these walls. She directed her household with an aristocratic calm as though she still lived in her native Seville. Hers was the unaffected warmth, the innate graciousness of the true patrician. She laughed with her eyes now as she listened to her husband's humming and reached over to place a hand upon his restless fingers.

On Don Porfirio's right was a young woman of startling beauty. She was blonde which, in itself, was enough to set her apart in a land that seemed to produce only variations of the brunette. Anna De Lacey. Austrian by birth. Her husband had been one of Maximilian's court and had been executed by a firing squad with Maximilian. There was a poise and regal detachment about her that she drew from somewhere beyond her twenty-three years. Her beauty was that of a flawlessly cut diamond resting alone upon a cushion of black velvet. She needed no setting. At her side, their chairs touching, was a man in the splendid, full-dress uniform of a Mexican general. Andre Corbel was a man whose big frame was deeply larded in the fat of indolence. His smile, when it came, was without meaning and the eyes behind it were shrewd and calculating. He lounged uncomfortably, his thick thighs seeming to push his legs apart. He watched the dancing without interest now and was sleepily indifferent to the conversation.

Standing behind the group, Sul tasted appreciatively the fine Havana of one of Don Porfirio's cigars, listened to the music and kept a watchful eye on his Rangers. There was a keg of *pulque* on a table with a gourd dipper. Now and then, with an affected casualness, the men moved to it, making wry faces at the taste but enduring it for the sake of its alcohol.

Turning her head, Anna De Lacey spoke to Sul. "Who," she asked with a faint, provocative accent, "is the handsome young one who stands there with your Rangers, Captain?"

"They're mostly young, Ma'm. And," he grinned, "I guess most of them think they're handsome."

"You're being evasive." She touched her lips with the tip of her fan. "You know very well the one I mean. The tall, handsome one who looks so very much like you. The resemblance is startling. He could be your brother."

"He is." Sul was uncomfortable beneath the extravagance of her phrasing and the indirect compliment.

Her eyes widened in genuine surprise. "The commander's brother and in the ranks?"

"He's a Ranger." Sul could not keep the pride from his voice. "That's rank enough."

"Well spoken, Captain." Don Porfirio smiled his approval. "Madame De Lacey is still too short a time away from the courts of Europe and poor Maximilian to understand our democracy."

"Ours, Don Porfirio?" Corbel seemed amused. "Don't tell me that you subscribe to this nonsense the Americans seem to cherish. That all men are created free and equal."

"But, General," Don Porfirio was gracious in his rebuke, "you forget that I am an American now. I have made my home here and these are my people. Would you want me to be on alien among them? If I do not yet believe it all, I can at least hope that it will come true."

Corbel inclined his head indifferently. "At least," he spoke softly and indicated the patio with an indolent wave of a hand, "it is good to see that you keep the old customs here in this new country of yours."

"Human nature does not change so much with the crossing of such a small river, even though it is called the Rio Grande," Dona Marguerita interposed smilingly. "We carry our customs with us but not, I hope, our prejudices. Have you not found it so, Madame De Lacey, in this new world of your choosing?"

"I am not in Texas entirely by choice, Senora." Anna De Lacey shrugged. "I cannot return to Mexico. I would be unwelcome in France or Austria. But, to be honest and at the risk of offending Don Porfirio, I find it a hideous country of rude manners, coarse men and faded women."

Corbel eyed her with an amused and almost patronizing familiarity. "Madame De Lacey, like all women, must have a mirror for her beauty. She has not found it in Texas."

Listening to the man, Sul was puzzled—not by the words, which were innocent enough, but by the faint undercurrent of malicious satisfaction that was difficult to define. It was the tone of a brutal man discussing a spirited horse to be broken.

There was a moment of constrained silence. Sensing she had offended her hosts Anna forced a quick change of manner with an apologetic laugh. "I am sorry if I seemed rude. It is only the uneasiness of all displaced persons who have had to start their lives anew in a strange country. Perhaps in time . . ." She permitted the sentence to remain incomplete.

Don Porfirio gravely examined the long, gray ash on his cigar. "I, also, have found it necessary to make small adjustments in my thinking. But this Texas, I believe, is worth it. One feels a tremendous vitality in the air with the simple crossing of a river. You step from one world into another. In time, I believe we shall see here a way of life so startlingly new that we cannot even begin to comprehend it now."

"If you survive the Indians, the bandits, the cattle thieves and mongrel packs of adventurers," Corbel blew softly between heavy lips.

"They come from both sides of the river, General." Sul could not resist the temptation.

Don Porfirio glanced at Sul with a quick smile of agreement. "Unfortunately, what you say is true. But, we shall survive, Captain. This Texas will grow and prosper and become peaceful through the efforts of such men as you and your Rangers. You have become that rare thing, my friend—a legend while still alive."

Sul laughed. "I'm afraid Texas already has too many legends, Don Porfirio. Almost any man with a fast gun can become a legend. A highwayman becomes a hero. Songs are written to extol the deeds of a murderer. Personally, I could do without so many legends. They keep me and my men chasing them down."

"What brings you to this part of the border, Captain?" Corbel asked the question with a lazy interest. "It is a far distance from your headquarters, is it not?"

"Our headquarters is usually where we unroll our blankets at night, General. This was a routine sweep but all of our trails usually end here at the Rio Grande."

"Such a small stream of water to cause so much trouble." Don Porfirio sighed. "Too many evil men on both sides find it too easy to cross."

"We try to make it harder, Don Porfirio." Sul was deliberately casual, hiding his impatience. "Mexico could make it easier for us by granting permission to cross over and take the thieves and cutthroats who find sanctuary there. Stolen cattle and outlaws cross and are out of our reach. Guns, ammunition and powder for the Indians pour in from Mexico."

"Are you suggesting there is a pattern in this exchange, Captain?" Corbel was amused. "An organized lawlessness in which Mexico is a partner?"

"Not Mexico, General." Sul kept his tone pleasantly conversational. "But a Mexican or Mexicans. I think it is a big operation behind a front of respectability. The roving bands of Comanches have no need for the number of cattle that are stolen every month in Texas. They could neither eat them nor graze them. What they could do is trade them for the things they want, guns and ammunition. Unorganized white rustlers couldn't dispose of thousands of head unless there was a point of distribution, a depot for their sale, a quick turnover for cash. Who is the man, or men, with the cash and the connections? He, or they, are either in Texas or across the river."

"You seem to point a finger, Captain, although I am not sure in which direction." Corbel was pleasantly interested.

"Neither am I, General." Sul frowned unconsciously. "But I am sure of this. If the old Indian alliances are reformed and cemented with enough guns then no one on your side of the river or ours will be safe."

"That, I should think, is a problem for your Army. *Verdad?*"

"The Army can't fight what it can't see, General." Sul realized Corbel was baiting him deliberately. "As a soldier you should know that."

"But the Rangers can?" Corbel's taunt was unmistakable.

With an effort, Sul held his temper in check. "No. But we can look a little harder, a little closer, before the trouble starts. If you cork up the jug the water won't spill." He turned to Dona Marguerita with an almost wistful smile of apology. "I am sorry we have intruded upon your fiesta."

"I have become accustomed to the fierce talk of men,

Captain." She shrugged good naturedly. "It is always so. Women speak only of their homes, their children. Men discuss fighting, cattle and money. Sooner or later both exhaust themselves."

"There is a proverb in Spanish." Corbel nodded in Sul's direction. "Even a hair casts its shadow. I assume that you seek the hair, Captain." His features drew themselves into a studied frown of regret. "I wish I could help. We do not welcome your bandits and murderers who cross into Mexico. We should be glad to get rid of them. However, granting you permission to enter Mexico and take them out by force intrudes upon such involved things as treaties and international law. They are beyond your authority or mine."

Sul inclined his head in agreement. "I understand that, General. But there is one thing you could do for us all. Find out who on your side ships great quantities of cattle to Cuba and who, with the return voyage, brings in large amounts of guns and ammunition."

"You seem determined to make this imaginary malefactor a countryman of mine, Captain." Corbel's tone had an undeniable edge.

"I don't know. Texans and Mexicans may not be working together, but together they are stirring up a big kettle of trouble. I don't want to see it boil over."

"Gentlemen," Dona Marguerita interposed firmly, "this conversation is becoming more suitable to a conference table than a fiesta."

Don Porfirio patted his hands softly and servants came immediately with earthenware jugs of cool wine to replenish the glasses. Sul caught Dona Marguerita's eyes and she smiled her forgiveness.

Within the patio, the tempo of music increased and several of the bolder Rangers moved in to take the slender, brown hands of the laughing girls. They stamped and whirled with more enthusiasm than grace and whooped their pleasure, sometimes leaping in the air to click their heels together.

Standing beside Pop, Yancey watched the dancers but too often his eyes strayed to the portal, drawn by the shining, crystal beauty of Anna De Lacey. He had never seen such a woman. An aura of grace hovered about her, seeming to illuminate the group. Her smile, the faint sound of her laughter, the movement of a hand or the turn of her head, were all fascinating. He was unaware of the intensity of his gaze until Pop's words startled him.

"She's something to look at, isn't she, boy? A woman to take a man's eyes."

Yancey grinned. "I didn't know it showed."

"That was a real, hungry look you had, like a hound staring at a bone out of reach on a shelf."

"You're a fraud, Pop." Yancey chuckled good-naturedly. "I have an idea you think up those little homilies to hide the truth: that you're an Eastern dude and probably a schoolmaster with no business in the Rangers." He turned again to the portal and saw Anna De Lacey touch Sul's arm with her fan and his brother lean over intimately to catch her words. He experienced a sensation of unreasonable resentment. Why should Sul be there with her, with Don Porfirio and the others?

As though he read the boy's thoughts Pop shook his grizzled head. "If you were a private in the Army, boy, you wouldn't expect to sit, drink and talk with the Captain, would you?"

"This isn't the Army." Even as he spoke Yancey was ashamed of his pique.

"You're wondering why Sul is there and not you. You're saying to yourself that there isn't any reason why you shouldn't be on the porch with Don Porfirio and his guests. The question doesn't become you, boy. Sul's your brother and a thing like this makes it harder for him than for you. It makes him a lonely man. Sure, he could ask you over but if he did that he'd have to do the same with the others. Now, except for you and, maybe Park, the boys just wouldn't be comfortable, but they'd sweat it out if Sul told them to."

"I guess so." Yancey admitted reluctantly.

"Rank has its privileges," the older man mused, "but it also has its obligations. That's something to remember when the going is tough and you want someone to lean on."

Bending over Anna De Lacey, Sul was aware of her soft and delicate fragrance. It disturbed him as did the soft, momentary touch of her hair against his cheek.

"Ask your brother to join us, Captain." It was a command, no less imperious for being gently phrased. "I should like to meet him. Or," and there was mischief in her eyes, "is it possible that you do not always carry your cherished democracy with you?"

Sul frowned. Damn women anyhow, he thought. They were always intruding into things they didn't understand, making it almost impossible to refuse them because of their deceptive, appealing manner. Not to grant the request would make him seem boorish and ill-humored.

"I ride with my men, fight with them." Unconsciously, he was defending himself against her charge. "We share the same blankets and the same food, the same discipline. It isn't a matter of caste, Ma'm, but of order."

"La! How stuffy you sound. Certainly, you would not be inviting chaos into your disciplined ranks by asking your own brother to meet us." Her next words were deliberately directed to Don Porfirio and Dona Marguerita. "I thought it would be pleasant if the Captain's brother joined us here."

Don Porfirio hesitated. He understood Sul's reluctance and yet an innate courtesy made it impossible for him to refuse the request of a guest. His eyes met Sul's and they seemed to shrug a good-humored apology.

"Of course, Captain." He inclined his head toward Anna. "We should be delighted. Your brother and the other Rangers, if you wish. By all means, call them."

Sul was trapped and angry. Why couldn't she mind her own business? It wasn't that he didn't want Yancey. Secretly, he had been proud of the boy over the past weeks. But he resented being forced into something he felt was irregular. He glanced across the patio and, catching Yancey's eye, made a beckoning motion. Yancey stared for a moment, and then, masking his pleasure, threaded his way through the dancers to the portal.

Sul was gravely impersonal making the introductions and Yancey, understanding that Sul's action had not been voluntary kept his face straight with an effort as he listened to his brother. It tickled him to see Sul caught in something he didn't like.

Anna De Lacey studied Yancey with interest, turning her gaze from brother to brother as though measuring them against each other. When she spoke, it was to Sul.

"How much alike you are and yet how different." It was a deliberate appraisal. "Did you, Captain, resemble your brother more completely when you first came to Texas?"

"I was younger, if that's what you mean." Deliberately, he pretended to misunderstand. This girl both irritated and attracted him.

"No—o!" She tilted her head to regard them both musingly. "That wasn't exactly what I meant. You look alike. There is the same manner, even a similarity of voice. It wouldn't be a matter of years alone but what they brought. I suspect Texas has changed you more than you realize, Captain."

The orchestra struck up a waltz. After a few halfhearted steps, the dancing Rangers gave up. They liked a tune to which a man could swing a girl until her skirts swirled to her knees and she spun on tiptoe. Reluctantly, they led their partners from the cleared space.

"Do you dance, Mr. Carter?" Invitingly, Anna De Lacey dropped the light reboza from her shoulders. "Do I call you Mr. Carter or Ranger Carter?" She ignored Corbel's petulant frown.

"Yancey would be fine, Ma'm." Privately he thought she was being pretty forward, asking a man to dance and all. But, maybe that was the way they did things in Texas. "I've been doing most of my dancing in a saddle these days but I'd like to try." He extended his hand and she placed hers lightly in it. Together, they crossed the portal and walked out upon the deserted court.

Swirling and dipping, feeling her as weightless as a windblown petal in his arms, Yancey was aware of their

audience. The servants, the appreciatively grinning
Rangers, the group on the portal.

"You dance well." Her words were softly pitched. "Is it
a requirement of the Rangers?"

"This is pure Virginia, Ma'm." He was enjoying himself.

As they twirled past the Rangers they suddenly heard
the warning whirr of a snake's rattle. The sound was so
sharp, so close that Yancey started and spun Anna De
Lacey abruptly away from it. Over her shoulder he saw
Park Manning absently trembling the dry cartilage between his fingers, staring innocently at the sky.

"That was a fool thing to do, Park." He made no effort
to disguise the anger.

"Please." Her fingers pressed lightly into his arm. "I
have lived long enough in Texas not to be frightened by
that sound."

He spun her away in time with the music. "He's like a
kid with a rattle. Plays with that fool thing all the time. I
never get used to it." The irritation ebbed slowly.

"It is a sound of warning, is it not?" She smiled up at
him. "Against me, perhaps?"

He looked down at her with astonishment. "That's a
funny thing to say."

The laughter was soft and bubbly in her throat. "Do
you take everything so literally, Mr. Carter? You are a
very serious man, are you not?"

The music stopped then and she took his arm with an
easy casualness. He felt the small pressure as he started to
lead her back to the portal. Expertly, she led him without
seeming to do so toward a far corner of the patio where a
fountain splashed softly beneath the overhanging, deep
purple blossoms of a jacaranda. There were thick clusters
of villa de noche and their fragrance was heavily sensual.

"That is a curious bloom, is it not, saving its perfume
for the night, hiding its beauty by day?" Her breath was a
sigh, her eyes heavy-lidded, almost as though she slept.

Before Yancey could think of a reply, she took a small
gold case from a bag. He watched with astonishment as
she selected a tipped cigarette. Without comment she

waited until Yancey recovered from his surprise and then held the tube between her lips, ready for the match. He fumbled in his pocket and then extended the flame toward her. By its light her eyes were cool, grave and speculative, her gaze on his face.

"Have you never seen a lady smoke a cigarette before, Mr. Carter?"

"Not a lady, Ma'm." The words were out before he thought.

She was not offended. "I assure you it is possible—to be a lady and still take an occasional cigarette."

"I—I didn't mean it just that way, Ma'm." The flame trembled between his fingers and he blew upon it hastily.

"Are you chilled or nervous, Mr. Carter?" The smoke escaped from between her parted lips.

"Nervous, I guess." He laughed without embarrassment. "I didn't know it showed though, Ma'm."

"You make me feel very old when you call me Ma'm." Her head tilted to one side, her eyes searching his face.

"Or me very young." He felt a little surer of himself. After all, she was only a girl and he'd known a lot of girls back in Virginia.

Across the night came the snarling cry of a cougar. It was a chilling sound that ended in a hoarse coughing. He felt her shiver.

"That's only a lonesome cat, looking for a mate."

"But he sounds so angry!"

"That's because he hasn't found her yet, Ma'm."

Her laughter was quick and lingered behind the quiet amusement in her eyes. "Perhaps you are not as young as I thought, Mr. Carter."

Behind them they could hear the scraping of chairs as Don Porfirio's party began breaking up. Anna De Lacey seemed indifferent to the sound or its implications.

"What would bring a man such as you to this country, Mr. Carter?"

"I've asked myself that question a few times during the past week. I guess it's just because I got tired of doing the same things as everyone else, the things that are expected of you back home."

"And you don't miss them—those things?" She seemed almost wistful.

"I haven't had time."

"Then you are more fortunate than you realize. I have too much time to remember, to think."

Through the jacaranda Yancey could see the good nights being exchanged on the portal and the figure of General Corbel, legs planted stubbornly apart, as he stared in their direction across the patio.

"I think everyone is leaving. Should I take you back? The General . . ." He left the sentence unfinished.

"Ah! Yes. The General." She seemed amused by the words. "I am certain he must be scowling our way. I can feel his displeasure from here. Unfortunately, it is not something to be borne lightly, but we shall risk it."

"Who is the General? I mean, what is he . . ." He stopped the question abruptly.

"What is the General to me, you were going to ask?"

"I—I guess so." He was miserably awkward. "I'm sorry. I don't know what made me say such a fool thing."

"Let me see," she mused. "This is a country of violence. I came to it alone, out of necessity. The General has been of great assistance. He is, let us say, my protector." She dropped the cigarette to the ground and set the satin toe of her slipper upon the red eye of its coal.

Yancey was shocked, wondering if she knew how the word "protector" sounded. Maybe, because she was a foreigner she said things without realizing what they meant. She appeared innocently young at this moment and yet there was a cool, ageless wisdom in her eyes.

"I have embarrassed you, haven't I, Mr. Carter?" She took his arm again. "Now you may take me to the house."

The patio was all but empty as they recrossed it. Only a few Rangers stood about the pulque. Yancey could feel their eyes as he led her to the deserted portal. There, in the shadows, she glanced up at him with a faint, sad smile and gave him her hand.

"My ranch is the San Sebastian. Your brother undoubtedly knows where it is. Perhaps, someday, you may find it convenient to stop by. I should like to see you again, Mr. Carter."

She left him then, quickly, and he could only stare after her with the uncomfortable feeling that for a second his mouth must have hung open in astonishment. A lady didn't say something like that to a man she had only met. They didn't in Virginia and he was pretty sure they didn't in Texas either. But she had said it. "I should like to see you again, Mr. Carter." He shook his head and turned away, recrossing the patio toward the wide gates, shaking off an invitation from the Rangers to come and have a drink.

Before the low, adobe structure that served the Rangers as a temporary barracks for the night, Sul and Park Manning stood in the semi-darkness talking.

"We'll ride out at daybreak." Sul blew on the end of his cigarette until its small cone glowed hotly. "What do you know about this Corbel?"

"Not much more than you. I just seem to remember that he's been real conspicuous in places where a lot of unpleasant things happened to other people, usually his friends. There was the assassination of Colonel Cruz in Senora. A tricked-up suicide of the Governor of San Luis Potosi. Corbel took over. There was a military junta that moved in on the presidente, in Mexico City. Corbel played on both teams. There's nothing really to put your finger on, but when you tie it all together he comes out a real shifty character."

Sul nodded. "What about this Anna De Lacey?"

Park pressed two fingers together and held them up for Carter's inspection. "Like that, from what I've heard. You know where her spread is, San Sebastian. It's never seemed like a working ranch, though. All of her hands are Mexican and there is a lot of traveling back and forth across the border. San Sebastian is one of the few places that has never been hit by rustlers. At least we've never had a complaint. That makes it unique, I'd say."

They both glanced up at the sound of footsteps. With a pleased grin, Yancey halted before them.

Sul inspected his brother. "You must be tougher than I

thought," he said dryly. "I figured you'd be ready for your bunk long before this."

"Mrs. De Lacey said she'd like a breath of fresh air." Yancey laughed softly. "Personally, I thought that was kind of funny since she'd been sitting in the fresh air all evening. Hey!" There was an animated note of incredulousness in his voice. "You know something? She smokes cigarettes, just like a man."

"Offhand," Sul kept a straight face, "I'd say that was about the only point of resemblance." He clapped Yancey on the back with rough affection. "We're riding into McNary early in the morning. Better get some sleep."

Unexpectedly, Yancey flared. "You going to start telling me when to go to bed?"

Sul regarded his brother gravely. The easy friendliness vanished. "Why, yes." The words came slowly, evenly. "I'm going to tell you when to go to bed, when to get up, when to ride and when to eat, just as I do every other Ranger in the company when we're on duty."

For a moment, the two stared at each other. Resentment fired the younger man's eyes. Watching them, Park thought unhappily that sooner or later these two were going to tangle. Yancey was tougher than he looked. It could be a real dinger of a hassle. Yancey refused to drop his gaze, continuing to meet Sul's eyes. Finally, he nodded curtly, swung about and disappeared inside.

Sul watched him go, then shook his head regretfully. "Ever have a kid brother, Park?"

"Nope." Manning made a reply although one was not called for.

"They never grow up." Sul whistled tunelessly.

"Oh! They usually do if you let them."

Sul wheeled to face him. "What's that supposed to mean?"

"That it is about time you forgot he was your brother. Not that you give it to him easy. I've watched you pile it on sometimes just because he is kin. Let him alone. He's just another recruit whose name happens to be Carter. That's the way I would handle it."

"I don't know what got into him." There was no anger

or resentment in Sul's musing. "He should have stayed back home in Virginia, finished school, married a nice girl, raised a family and amounted to something. That's what the Carters are supposed to do. That's what they've been doing for a long time."

"All except Sullivan Carter. He's different. He can do as he damn well pleases. Is that it?"

Sul's slow grin was embarrassed. He scratched at his ear and regarded Park with a chuckle. "I guess so. Thanks, Park." He turned and, stooping to avoid the lintel, ducked inside the darkened barracks. Manning finished his cigarette thoughtfully.

Chapter Eight

The main street of McNary was pressed flat beneath the sun's hot iron. A few people walked it listlessly, stopping now and then in the shade of a building's overhang to mop at their faces and stare accusingly at the burnished sky.

The hooves of the Rangers' horses rang on the flinty earth as they moved, two abreast, along the rutted path. They reined in before a long hitching rail and dismounted, slapping irritably at the dust which covered them. Then, to a man except Sul, they headed directly for the moistly dim recess of a cantina.

Sul stood beside the rail taking an unnecessarily long time with the loop of his reins. His eyes searched up and down the nearly empty street. Then he turned away and strode along the boardwalk toward a frame building over which hung a faded sign: City Marshal. Justice of the Peace. Juzgado. Policia.

Leaning against the weathered frame, a ragged, dirty Indian swayed drunkenly. A doltish grin was fixed upon his face and his head lolled back and forth, jerking now and then as he tried to steady it. As Sul passed before him, the Indian pitched helplessly, falling heavily against the Ranger, clutching frantically at his shirt in an effort to keep on his feet. With a rough shove Sul slammed him back against the building. Instead of dropping to the ground the Indian bounced from the sheathing, falling against the Ranger again with a force that almost sent them both to the boardwalk in a hopeless tangle. Sul whipped his hand against the vacant face and for a second the dark eyes glittered with anger.

From their places in tilted chairs before the store fronts a few loungers rose with cackling grins to watch the fun. They crowded with avid curiosity about Sul and the drunk, waiting to see what the Ranger was going to do.

The Indian sagged, his knees buckling, and Sul reached down to jerk him upright. Then he turned angrily to the crowd.

"Where did this Indian get whiskey?"

No one answered. The men returned Sul's accusing stare with indifference. Carter jerked at the Indian's flimsy shirt and whirled him about. With a shove he propelled the staggering drunk toward the marshal's open door, and the spectators moved up to watch. Sul turned and slammed the door shut in their faces and they sidled up to peer through the windowpane.

Tom Hayden, McNary's marshal, rose heavily from behind a scarred and littered table. He eyed Sul and the Indian morosely.

"Now you know I ain't got no place for a drunken Indian, Sul. What you want to bring him in here for?"

Without replying Sul took a key from a nail on the wall, pushed the Indian toward the single cell and locked the barred door. The Indian collapsed soundlessly into a corner, looking at Carter reproachfully.

"I don't want no Indian stinkin' up my jail." Hayden objected feebly. "Suppose I get me a real customer, what then?"

Sul replaced the key, pushed a litter of papers away from a corner of the table and sat on it. He grinned at the marshal.

"This place couldn't stink any worse than it does," he
said agreeably. "Let him sleep it off. He'll only get into
trouble out there on the street. Someone will start to horse
him around and the first thing you know there'll be a
knifing. Then you'll have to go out in that hot sun and
bury him." He glanced casually through a pile of old
Wanted circulars.

Hayden glanced from the Ranger to the dozing prisoner
and nodded resignedly. "If you say so, Sul." He stood,
fingering his protruding belly, scratching absently. "What
brings you into McNary?"

"Just exercising the horses." Sul smiled faintly. "They
were going stale, standing around in the stables doing
nothing. How are things with you?"

"Nothin' much ever happens here an' you know it. Just
the usual amount of Saturday night hell-raisin'." Hayden
plucked at his sweat-stained shirt and blew hopefully
down the opening across damp skin. "Old man Barstow
was burned out, I hear."

Sul nodded wearily. "We came through his place a
couple of days back."

"Looks like things are gettin' worse all the time," Hayden said almost cheerfully. "Fellow named Hinton came
in today. Said some brush thumpers hit his place, roughed
up his wife an' ran the stock off. I tell you this whole
section's spooked. People are just givin' up an' movin'
away. It's like a plague or somethin' that no one knows
the cure for."

Sul's eyes clouded. Fear and insecurity held the entire
border. Sudden death and destruction were commonplace.
Men and their families lived in terror from day to day and
the evil mounted. Except for the larger settlements, the
local authority was represented by such tired hacks as
Hayden, comfortable and complacent in a steady job. An
occasional drunk was all they cared to handle and so the
lawless ran free and wild. He sighed and moved from the
desk to drop tiredly into a chair. The marshal went to the
window and stared out across the street. Sul half-smiled to
himself.

"I'll be around for a while, Tom," he suggested idly. "If you want to duck out for a spell I'll keep shop for you."

The marshal popped his lips. "I was just thinkin' that I might have a little touch." For the first time he came to life. Grabbing his hat, he went to the door. "Just call me when you're ready to leave."

Sul watched as the man lumbered hastily across the street and through the swinging doors of a saloon. For a minute there was silence in the room.

"You got a mighty heavy hand, Sul." The words came distinctly from the cell.

Carter didn't turn his head but a tiny smile creased his face. "How are you Charley?" He spoke without turning.

The man stood close to the bars. "Tired of playin' Indian an' you didn't have to be so convincin' with that roughin' up out there."

"I wanted it to look good."

"That sure isn't the way it felt."

Sul tilted his chair back against the wall, watching the street outside. "What have you found out?"

"Not much more than we already knew. Somethin's got into the Indians. They're countin' sticks in every Comanche and Kiowa village. They're mixin' the black paint in the hills and they're gettin' guns, lots of 'em, a few at a time."

"Who's supplying them?" Sul half-turned to stare at the man in the cell.

"It ain't even a name. The cattle get drove over at night, then small parties of Indians cross an' pick up the guns. Everybody seems to know just what to do, where an' when. This is kind of different than what we've been used to, Sul." There was grave concern in the statement. "It ain't just some crazy Indians hellin' around without a purpose. They're bein' fed a lot of talk about how Texas is goin' to be taken away from the whites an' given back to the tribes so it's all Indian land again. That kind of stuff makes big tobacco for the chiefs to smoke. They like the taste of it real well."

Sul hit his hand against his knee. "We've got to find out

who runs this show, who's making the promises, who's behind the trade. If we don't we're goin' to see a massacre the like of which no one can imagine. You're going to have to stay with this a while longer, Charley."

"I guess so. You know somethin', Sul?"

"What?"

"I worry." The admission was dolefully accented. "I worry a lot lately about gettin' bald. On a job like this, a man can lose all his hair in about a minute, if he's unlucky."

"Well, you stay lucky, Charley." The legs of the chair hit the floor with a thud. "The Marshal's coming back now."

"How long do I have to stay in here? I sure could use a drink an' some tobacco."

"I'll tell Hayden to let you out at sundown. Likely enough he'll turn you loose just as soon as I leave. Do you need any money?"

"What'd I use money for?" There was outrage in the question. "Indians are real underprivileged characters, Sul. I can't buy nothin', can't do nothin'."

Sul rose as the marshal came puffing through the doorway. The man glanced at the sleeping Indian and frowned.

"How long do I have to keep him around, Sul?"

"Turn him loose in a few hours." The Ranger was casually indifferent. "I just didn't want him getting into trouble." He extended his hand. "It was good to see you again, Tom. Take care of yourself."

"I sure aim to do just that." Hayden dropped into a chair. "Where you bound for now?"

"Brownsville."

"You got it real good." The marshall spoke enviously. "Go wherever you want, whenever you want. Me, I don't get to go no place but across the street."

"We can't all be lucky." Carter agreed gravely. "Like you say, some folks get it easy. Well, so long." He moved from the room without a glance at the cell and passed out of sight beyond the window.

The cantina was a dim, low room with a few crudely-wrought chairs and unsteady tables on the earthen floor. There were no dancing girls, no mirrors behind the bare pine bar, no piano, no brass spittoons. Dogs, chickens and an occasional pig wandered in from the back yard. At one of the tables in a corner Park Manning, Pop and Yancey spread their arms about small glasses of tequila. The rest of the Rangers lounged at the bar, making a serious and silent business of their drinking. Sul kicked out a chair, poured himself a drink from a half-filled bottle, took a lick of salt, swallowed and absently sucked on half a lime.

"I had a talk with Indian Charley." He answered Park's unasked question. "But he doesn't know much more than we do. Someone, meaning you Park, has got to go across the river and stay there for a while. I want to know who's getting the stolen cattle and trading guns in return."

"That's a big order, Sul." Park eyed his superior unhappily.

Sul nodded agreeably. "That's why I need a big man for the job. Take someone with you. Go into Matamoros from Brownsville. I don't know where to tell you to start looking."

"All right." Manning's glance swept the room and then settled upon Yancey. "I'll take Yancey with me."

"No." Sul shook his head.

"Why not?" Yancey swung about to face his brother.

"If Park runs into trouble he'll need someone with experience he can count on. I know how you feel, but you aren't ready yet."

"I never will be if you have your way. How do I get experience, tied to your halter like an unweaned calf? I'm getting pretty sick and tired of this, Sul."

"Not half as sick as you would be with a knife or a slug in your belly."

"I signed to do a Ranger's job. I want to do it." Yancey stood up, almost as though he dared his brother to rise.

"I'll take my chances with him, Sul." Manning watched the dark anger spread across Yancey's face.

Sul shook his head. "You'll be taking enough chances as it is. Don't stack the odds against yourself."

Yancey grabbed at his brother's shoulder, half-spinning him around. "Sul, captain or no captain, one of these days we're going to have a real go 'round."

"I suppose so." Sul ignored the clutching hand. The agreement was reluctant. "It isn't something I'm looking forward to, I'll tell you that." He shrugged his shoulder out from Yancey's grasp. "It still won't change anything as long as I'm running this troop. This isn't something I like doing. You've got a lot of things to learn and it takes time. I just don't want your education to be at someone else's expense."

The figure of a man in the doorway blocked out the sunlight. A scraggly beard covered his face. His eyes were sunken and red-rimmed. His clothing was dusty, and lines of fatigue were carved into his face.

"Which of you is Ranger Carter?" The words were half-choked.

Sul turned from Yancey. "I'm Carter."

With a shuffling gait the man moved across the floor until his face was inches away from Sul's. He wiped at his dry mouth with the back of a trembling hand.

"I heard you were in town. My name's Hinton." The eyes turned accusingly to the men at the bar. "I wanted to see for myself with all that trouble goin' on how you Rangers can sit around drinkin' an' carousin'."

"There's not much drinking, Mr. Hinton, and very little carousing, as you call it."

"I lost me a hundred an' fifty head of cattle last night." The voice rose to an almost hysterical pitch. "Everything I had in the world is gone. I look to the Rangers for help an' find 'em layin' around in a bar. People just don't care no more what happens to folks." He was on the verge of unashamed tears.

"I'm sorry about your cattle, Mr. Hinton, but we can't be every place." Sul's voice was quietly soothing.

"And I'm sick of that word 'sorry'." Hinton almost screamed his frustration. "The Indians raid a wagon train, burn a settlement an' the Army is sorry. A man is robbed of all he's got, his wife taken like a squaw by some rustlers an' the Rangers is sorry." He jabbed a finger into Sul's chest. "A dollar a day, hard money, that's what you Rangers get for layin' around here, drinkin' an' laughin'."

"It's been a long time since I laughed and meant it, Mr. Hinton."

"You're supposed to be the law in Texas." Outrage caused the man's voice to tremble. "Well! If you are, then it ought to be a place where a man can amount to somethin', raise a family an' not have to sleep with a gun beside him. Why don't you make it so, Ranger? Tell me that!"

"We keep trying, Mr. Hinton." Sul poured a glass full of tequila and handed it to the man. For a moment Hinton seemed on the point of knocking the drink from the Ranger's hand. Then he sagged and took the drink, gulping it down.

"I'm sorry, Ranger." The apology came wearily. "I guess you do the best you can, but it ain't near enough. A man can only take so much an' then he's got to blame someone. I'm cleaned out. My wife's hurt bad."

"What's your brand?" Sul motioned toward the bottle but Hinton shook his head. "The chances are your stock is across the river by now but I'd still like to know."

"A broken H." Hinton began to laugh. "That's real good, ain't it? A broken H. That's what I am now, broke." He stared helplessly into Sul's face and then turned and shuffled toward the door and was gone.

The silence in the cantina was broken only by the buzzing flies, the bony thumping of a dog's leg as it scratched its fleas. The Rangers stared at the vacant doorway.

"Dewey." Manning's voice was curt as he singled out one of the men. "Finish your drink. We're going for a ride."

The man, Dewey, stared his astonishment. "I just had me a ride, Park."

"This one is going to be real instructive." Manning shifted his gun belt. "Foreign travel." He turned to Sul as Dewey reluctantly picked up his hat from the bar. "How am I going to get word to you?"

"You'll have to find me. I'll leave word here and there.

You're not going to have any law behind you, Park.
You're not even supposed to be in Mexico, so if you get
into trouble you'll have to work it out yourselves." He
paused thoughtfully, "We'll be in and out of Willow Bend.
Let's plan on meeting there. That's about as definite as I
can make it. If you find out anything come back over and
wait until we show up. Right now I'd like to see if we can
find the spot where Hinton's cattle were driven across. It
may give us a lead on the direction they travel." He
paused and then extended his hand. "Good luck and be
careful."

Chapter Nine

Sul rode slowly from the mesquite- and cac-
tus-studded plateau toward the growth of willows, tangled
brush and cottonwood. He knew a thousand head of cattle
could be driven along this route without leaving much of a
trail. Working north and south along the river, the other
Rangers were trying to find the fording spot. Anger drove
Sul. Drawing up within the dappled shade of the cottonwood grove he felt cheated, outwitted, helpless. The mem-
ory of Hinton's stricken features would not be erased. He
was pitted against shadows that ran and disappeared before they could be recognized. Pushing back his hat with a
forearm he stared at the sky and a hidden voice riveted
him in that position.

"I'm right behind you, Sul." The words were a malicious chuckle, harsh and triumphant. "I wouldn't move
none if I was you."

Sul knew the voice. "What do you want, Latham?"

"Now you know good an' well what I want." The tone
was reproachful. "I want you, Carter. I been wantin' you
just like this for a long time. Now!" The word was crisp.

"Hook those guns out with your little fingers an' let 'em fall to the ground."

Slowly, carefully, Carter did as he was ordered.

"For a man who's not used to takin' orders you're doin' just fine." Latham was approving. "Now, pull out the rifle with your left hand an' let it fall with the others." The rifle came out of the scabbard and dropped with a soft thud. "That's good, that's real good." The compliment ended in a laugh. "Nudge your horse a little, Sul, until he's under that big limb there. Do it easy 'cause you know he ain't near as fast as a bullet. I'd hate to shoot you, Sul an' spoil what can be a first-rate hangin'."

At the pressure of Sul's knee the horse looked back with curiosity and then obediently sidled toward a tree until Sul checked him beneath a stout limb.

"I was in McNary today when you all come ridin' in. I heard about old man Hinton goin' to see you. Knowin' you for the kind of a fella you are, I figured you to go ridin' off, looking for the cattle tracks. You ain't very careful, Sul. I been followin' you for most an hour. It don't pay to be careless. No, sir, it just sure don't."

Somewhere along the river a crow sounded its rasping, croaking note. A twig broke under the pressure of a small, unseen animal. Above them, Latham's breathing was heavy as he labored triumphantly under the excitement of the moment. Sul waited, his mouth a thin, angry line.

"Put your hands behind your back, Carter." Latham was directly behind him now and the rifle jabbed viciously into his ribs.

As his hands came back, Sul wondered grimly how he was going to get out of this. A loop of rawhide tightened around one wrist and then the other, securing them together. The pressure of the rifle eased as Latham carefully backed his horse away. There was a sound of movement, the shaking out of a rope and then its soft whistle as it was lofted up over the branch.

"The Rangers will hunt you down for this, Latham. No matter where you go or how you try to hide, someone will follow." Sul's mouth was dry.

"I'll take my chances. You killed my boy, Carter. I'm

goin' to hang you for it, hang you the way you did him. Only it's goin' to take a little longer."

A loop settled over Sul's head, hung slackly about his neck for a moment and then was drawn taut. The horse moved nervously beneath him and Sul whispered soothingly to it. He heard Latham dismount and from the corners of his eyes saw him make the free end of the rope fast to a second limb. The man tested it with a grunt of satisfaction. Then he swung back into the saddle and walked his mount until the two faced each other. His eyes were small points of hate and satisfaction.

"I'm goin' to leave you here this a-way, Carter. Sooner of later that horse of yours is goin' to move. He'll inch a piece at a time, grazin', an' the rope'll get tighter an' tighter on your neck. Maybe somethin'll scare him an' he'll bolt. Maybe, after a while, he'll get thirsty an', smellin' the river, will amble off. For a while, maybe you can hold him still by talkin' but sooner or later he'll go and when he does he's goin' to leave you hangin' in the air. I'd like to see that but I can't wait around. I could quirt him now an' have it over with but, somehow, I like this better. It ain't often a man can get hung by his own horse." The laugh split his mouth open and the yellow, broken teeth were wolfish. He wheeled and spurred his animal, and the sudden movement caused Sul's horse to half-rear.

Sul listened to the soft, crunching sound of the hooves as they grew distant and faded. Slowly, the small sounds of the brush reasserted themselves. A blue jay swooped to land on a swaying clump of mesquite. A brittle twig crackled. A lizard slithered past with a bright flash of striped color. A hawk cruised the sky with silent watchfulness and a blue-bottle fly circled with an excited buzzing. The horse, after a moment of waiting, bent its head to the ground, cropping at the short, wiry grass. The movement tightened the noose about Sul's neck, gagging him. He strained backward uncomfortably to relieve the tension. The fly settled on the animal's withers and the skin rippled nervously.

Desperately, Sul tried to think of a way out. This was one hell of a way to die. He thought of yelling but was afraid of startling the horse. He made soft, clucking sounds, whispering to the beast while his mind sought frantically for some way of release. He realized how imminent and real the danger was. The horse was an obedient and well-trained animal but sooner or later it would move, as Latham had predicted. Already the rough strands of the rope were chafing his throat, making a burning wale, and it was difficult to swallow. Again the horse moved a couple of inches and Sul raised himself in the stirrups, balancing uneasily in an effort to take the strain from the rope. He raged in his helplessness and strained in an effort to free his imprisoned hands. As the minutes lengthened and the hot cording about his neck became almost unbearable, he had a wild impulse to kick into the horse's side and have it over with. He was being strangled slowly and dared not stand in the stirrups for fear of losing his balance. Once out of the saddle he was finished. He tried to swallow and couldn't.

Working along the river, Yancey looked over to the opposite bank. Across the narrow stream lay Mexico. The knowledge stirred him although there was nothing about it that seemed different from the soil on which he stood. It was a land of dark and bloody history written, in part, by a lonely and baffled man named Cortez. Cortez, the man who once stopped to weep beside a tree on the outskirts of Mexico City for a dream unfulfilled. If Sul hadn't interfered Yancey would be on his way now, riding with Park Manning. Resentment against Sul rankled in him. One of these days, he promised himself. One of these days I'll show him.

He had purposely drifted away from the other Rangers because he felt the need to be alone. Now, he allowed his horse to stand in the shallow, rippling water while he stared across the river. Thinking of Mexico, he found himself connecting it with Andre Corbel and, inevitably, Anna De Lacey. San Sebastian. He wondered where it was and what she did in this lonely country. It was funny, a woman, a girl really, living by herself on a ranch miles from anywhere. He grinned to himself. Mooning over

Anna De Lácey wasn't finding where Hinton's cattle had crossed.

He turned from the river's edge and moved slowly through the scraggly growth toward a slightly wooded rise. The ears of his mount flicked nervously and it nickered. Yancey drew him up to look cautiously about. There was no sign of anyone else. He nudged the animal forward and the horse whinnied again. Feeling just a little foolish and self-conscious, Yancey drew his gun. Far in the distance he could hear the shout of one of the Rangers. They were up river a mile or so but the sound was surprisingly distinct. Again Yancey's horse whinnied and was answered by an animal somewhere within the stand of cottonwood.

"Hey?" Yancey shouted the question.

Sul heard the hail with relief and embarrassment. It was bad enough to be found this way by any of the men but Yancey would never let up on it. This was a fine way to be caught by a kid brother you were trying to teach to be a Ranger.

"Hey?" The shout came again.

"Yancey? Over here." He forced a strangled reply.

Yancey reholstered his revolver. Except in practice he had never fired it. "That you, Sul?"

The reply was oddly gurgled and unintelligible but it served as a guide. Yancey pushed through the brush and then halted, his mouth slackly open with an expression of complete astonishment. Then he began to laugh while Sul twisted uncomfortably to glare at him.

"Grandma used to tie a goose up like that to get it ready for the oven." Yancey shook his head with mock admiration.

Sul's horse moved companionably toward the newcomer and Sul's reply was abruptly shut off by an agonized strangle. Shaking his head with feigned astonishment Yancey moved, edging Sul's mount back until the strain was taken from the rope. Sul could only glare with red-faced impotence.

"I guess a man could ride Texas for years," Yancey marveled, "and never find a real, experienced captain of the Rangers in a fix like this. I declare, but it is going to be a story to tell around the saloons and cracker barrels and that's a fact." He mimicked a Texas drawl.

"Stop behaving like a simpering fool and cut me down." The words came with difficulty.

"I think I'd better ask my brother about that." Yancey replied doubtfully. "He's going to be upset enough as it is, me being off alone this way. You see," he leaned forward confidentially, "I'm new to this country. It does beat all, though, how a man could get himself tied up this way." Deliberately he rode in a small circle, admiring his brother from all sides. "You're kind of like a bomb, aren't you, ready to go off any minute?" The question was voiced with innocent admiration.

"Are you going to get this rope from around my neck or talk us both to death?"

"Well, I don't know." Yancey was doubtful. "Maybe I ought to go and get some of the other boys to help me. It's kind of a big job for a greenhorn to tackle. A real captain of the Texas Rangers!" He whistled a note of awe. For a moment more he sat, leaning forward in the saddle, regarding his fuming brother with quizzical delight. Then, he loosened the knot and slipped the noose over Sul's head. With a knife he slashed the buckskin thong at the wrists. "We ought to make a little deal over this, Sul," he suggested. "From now on you treat me as a man. You forget I'm your brother and I'll forget this."

Sul nodded, rubbing tenderly at his chafed throat. "Rale Latham." He said.

"All by himself and you with three guns?" Yancey indicated the ground.

"All by myself and with three guns that I never had a chance to use." Sul snapped the reply and jerked his horse around with unnecessary roughness. He dropped to the ground, retrieved the revolvers and rifle. "I know Latham. He won't stop now. Sooner or later I'll have to kill him. It isn't something I want to do. Come on." He mounted. "Let's ride."

Chapter Ten

They moved in single file across the silently running river. Where the moon laid a shaft of light, the passage of the horses threw up a small shower of silver. The all but naked bodies glistened like rubbed copper and the dyed feathers on their lances fluttered in the night's breeze.

From their places of concealment along a boulder-strewn ledge the Rangers watched them pass. This was no war party bent on a swift raid into Mexico. The band was too small for that, no more than a dozen. At the column's head one Indian bulked hugely on a small pony. His chest swelled out from beneath the soft buckskin shirt, making him look oddly out of proportion. He was the only one so covered. The others wore only a breechclout. The face, with a sharply beaked nose, was framed between two lank braids of hair. He sat his mount with a stiff pride and as he entered the water kept his eyes steadfastly on the opposite shore.

"That's old Iron Shirt," Sul whispered to Yancey who was flat beside him. "I'd give a hell of a lot to know where he's going and who he's meeting."

Yancey was tight with excitement. These were the first hostile Indians he had ever seen. "Why don't we whack into them?"

"You just can't shoot up a dozen Indians because they decide to take a ride in the moonlight." Sul was stripping himself of the heavy boots, trousers and shirt. "But I'm going across and see where they go."

"I'm going with you." Yancey tugged at his boots.

For a moment, Sul was about to shake his head. Then, something in Yancey's expression stopped him. He grinned slowly and nodded. "Leave your guns here. It isn't deep enough to swim. We'll have to crawl through the shallows."

"You going without horses?" Yancey was astonished.

"I don't think they're going far. I have a feeling it's a meeting just over the river."

When the last of the Indians had disappeared into the darkness on the opposite shore Sul whispered quick instructions to the other Rangers. Then he and Yancey moved away and down into the river. Yancey grinned at the spectacle of his brother, his neck and wrists banded by a deep tan while the rest of his body was almost indecently white. For his part, he felt completely vulnerable. There was nothing quite so calculated to destroy a man's confidence as taking his pants away from him. He was surprised to realize how defenseless he felt without a gun; how much a part of him a revolver had become in so short a time.

The first shock of the water, no more than three of four feet deep in spots, was numbing. Sul appeared oblivious to the discomfort. On his belly, he began wiggling across the sharp stones, barely covered by water in places.

"We look like a couple of things that have crawled out from under the rocks," he whispered to Sul. "What are those things, salamanders, I guess, that are supposed to go through fire and water?"

Sul only grunted softly. His eyes searched the indistinct shore for a sign of a sentry or rear guard. He sank into a deep hole and his feet churned soundlessly, carrying him through it and again into shallow water.

Breathless from the chill and excitement, Yancey pulled himself up on the bank beside Sul who was pressed flat on the shore. Then, at a nod, he moved half-crouched through the tangle that tore at his skin and over rocks that bit viciously at his tender feet.

At the muffled sound of voices Sul froze, located the direction and, after a moment, moved stealthily toward it. They found scant cover, taking advantage of it wherever they could, but for the most part they were in the open, inching forward on their bellies. The voices were louder now, the words in Spanish but unintelligible at this dis-

tance. A horse whinnied. The voices halted abruptly but
after a pause continued. Sul jerked his head toward a large
bush and they raced, bent over, to its concealment.

Peering through the ragged tangle, they gazed upon a
curious tableau. The Indians, drawn into a single line, sat
their mounts impassively. Confronting them, separated by
a few yards, was a similar grouping of riders. Facing
each other, the muzzles of their horses almost touching,
were the chief, Iron Shirt, and Andre Corbel.

Sul sucked in his breath, caught the look of astonishment on Yancey's face and nodded grimly.

Iron Shirt's eyes ranged over the horsemen and his lips
pressed into a bitter line. When he spoke again his words
were sharp, suspicious, rebuking.

"Where are the guns you promised?"

"Where are the men to use them?" Corbel's reply was
contemptuous.

"The warriors of four tribes are gathered in idleness in
many places waiting for you to put rifles in their empty
hands," Iron Shirt answered impatiently.

"I have given my word." Corbel spoke distinctly. "You
will have the rifles, the powder, the bullet metal for pour-
ing, but to pay for these things I must have more cattle."

In the half-light, Sul and Yancey could see the spasm
of derision as it crossed Iron Shirt's face.

"You are a small man to carry with him so much
greed." The insult was a lash.

Corbel stiffened. "And you speak with the impatience
of a boy. Give me this, give me that."

Yancey pressed his mouth close to Sul's ear. "Do you
understand what they're saying?"

Sul nodded and put a finger warningly to his lips.
"Most of it," he whispered.

Iron Shirt's words were ringingly clear. "I have learned
many things from the white men, but not yet to beg. I do
not trust you. I do not like you." He seemed on the point
of turning his horse away.

Corbel's attitude became a shade more conciliatory.
"Must the flint like the stone before, together, they kindle
a great fire?"

"There is truth in that." Iron Shirt nodded approvingly, the Indian's love for imagery caught by the phrase.

"Then," Corbel pressed the small advantage, "let us strike upon each other until the flames of our anger envelop Texas. We will drive the Anglos out and all of their lands will be returned to your people."

"If you do not lie about the guns, my people will fight beside you for such a cause."

"I do not lie." Corbel's answer was proud.

"Then we will find more cattle for which to pay for the guns and powder. But who is to say when you have had enough, when we have done our share? Already the border has been stripped for many miles back. We must range farther and farther to find large herds. The whites are more watchful than ever, the Rangers ride constantly and even the Army seeks to pen us up."

"With the guns you will be able to deal with all of them."

For a moment, Iron Shirt thought this over and then he nodded. "I will call our people together and tell them what you have said. Only," the Indian leaned forward, "do not forget your promise. If you take the cattle and do not deliver the guns we will cross your little river and hunt you down in your own country. It will not hold us back."

With a swift rearing of his mount he turned and the line of Indians parted to give him passage. Corbel and his men waited until the sound of their river crossing was audible. Then they turned in the opposite direction and disappeared into the night.

"Son of a gun!" Sul whispered almost admiringly. "He really sold those Indians a gold brick." Rapidly, he sketched for Yancey the conversation between Corbel and Iron Shirt. "And," he concluded, "there isn't much we can do about Corbel as long as he stays in Mexico. Even if he comes across," he admitted grudgingly, "he's pretty safe unless we can catch him at something, and that isn't likely. The Indians do the stealing. He collects the profits."

They made their way back across the river. As they

dressed, Sul outlined to the other Rangers what had happened.

"I'm going to ride to Fort Clark and see if I can talk some sense into the Army. If Corbel isn't lying about the shipment of guns and powder, we've got to stop the wagons from crossing over. There are a hundred fording places along the river and it's going to spread us thin, trying to cover them all. Johnson, you and Clifton will have to go back to Davis. Send someone to Austin to tell them what is about to happen. Bring back as many men with you as they can spare." His eyes swept over the crescent of men. "I'll take Pop and," the hesitation was barely perceptible, "Yancey. The rest of you set up some sort of a camp at Willow Bend and wait for us there. If Park shows tell him what's happening. Indian Charley should be along if he has anything new to report. I guess that's about all." He smiled faintly. "Keep your eyes open and your hair on."

Seeing to his gear, checking his guns, Yancey marveled, as he often did, at the casualness with which these men accepted their assignments; a long, dangerous ride to Austin, the backbreaking trip to Davis. Hostility hedged them on all sides. He chuckled suddenly as he realized he, also, had come to regard these things as routine. He had only the vaguest idea where Fort Clark was or how long it would take to get there. Distance was no longer a matter of miles but of days or weeks. Yet, here he was, saddling up, laying out blanket, canteen, food and guns as though he were setting out on a pleasure trip. The Rangers, he realized, did their work well.

He was in the saddle and waiting when Sul and Pop mounted. There were no last-minute instructions to those left behind. Sul knew his men and, in a situation such as this, had no need to issue orders. His easy "so long" was no more than he might have said on leaving them to cross a street. He glanced up at the clear sky for a moment, nodded and then nudged his animal into motion. Pop and Yancey fell in beside him. Then there was only the creak of leather, an occasional tinkle of metal, the crunching

sound of the hooves on brittle grass and scrub. The great
silence of the night dropped about them like a tent.

Sul was deep in his own thoughts. He tried to measure
the threat of the Indians, well armed and mounted, filled
with the dream of driving the white man out forever.
Andre Corbel? Greed inflamed the man; greed and ambition were twin goads. He could work quietly and in
security across the border. Who knew what grandiose
ideas filled his head? Did he honestly think he could wrest
Texas from American hands and set himself up as an
Emperor of the land? It was fantastic, but history was
filled with the improbable and bloody wars that had been
started with less hope of success. As allies he could call
upon what was probably the best cavalry in the world.
The horse had released the Indian from a foot-dragging,
static existence and transformed him into a reckless no-
mad who traveled swiftly and lightly. Well armed and
supplied, nursing a hatred for the whites who had taken
his land and driven him out like an animal, the Indian
would rage along the border with the fury of a wind-
driven prairie fire. That, in the end, he could not win was
a thought that would not enter his mind. Each day's
triumph would be sufficient to carry him into the next. He
thought of what an Indian chief had once said to him. The
old man, squatting in the dirt before his lodge, had looked
up at the Ranger. "The world is so large," he mused,
"with so much room for all, how is it possible that the
white man makes it small with his greed?"

Dawn came with a slate gray sky in which the stars
grew pale and vanished in small clusters. In the leaden
clouds to the east the sky seemed to break open as a
halved opal and the day about them was suddenly filled
with the sharp, small cries of unseen birds as though a
great cage had suddenly been opened. A light, moist wind
drifted past and the heat from the growing sun drove the
night's chill away. There was the sweet scent of damp
grass, the acrid and, not unpleasant, ammoniac smell of
the horses.

Within the shelter of a spiked shield of cactus, they

halted to make a small, smokeless fire. They boiled strong coffee to wash down dry biscuits and thick strips of raw bacon which they chewed and swallowed contentedly without talking. Pop finished breakfast with a chew from a black twist while Sul and Yancey rolled cigarettes.

"We can probably make Clark in a two-day ride." Sul rose and stretched, staring at the sky from which the wisps of cloud were being driven by the sun.

"Do you think they'll listen to you, boy?" Pop looked up at him.

"They'll listen. West Point teaches its officers tact and politeness." Sul half-smiled. "Whether they'll do anything more than listen is something else again. The military mind is punitive rather than precautionary." He whistled softly, thoughtfully for a moment. "San Sebastian, the De Lacey ranch, lies across our way. I was thinking of putting in there for the night. It'll give the horses a rest and, since this Corbel business, the lady interests me. You remember her, don't you, Yancey?" he concluded innocently. "The one who smokes cigarettes like a man?"

Yancey squirmed uncomfortably. "She seemed like a real nice lady; a girl, really. I don't see her being mixed up with a fellow like Corbel."

"A general, even a Mexican general, can do a lot of favors. This is a lonely country and people take help where they can get it." Sul spoke idly. "It just could be that San Sebastian is the ranch I've been looking for, right under my nose all the time."

Yancey's jaw tightened stubbornly. "I don't believe it. I don't believe she knows what Corbel is up to."

"Maybe not." Sul cinched the saddle girth. "But, it won't do any harm to drop in on her. Might even get in a waltz or two." He winked at Pop while Yancey muttered unintelligibly.

As the morning lengthened, the sun became a relentless tormentor. It followed them in shimmering waves until the heat all but sucked the air from their lungs. Men and animals drooped beneath it. The only breeze was that created by the movement of the horses. It was near noon when they came upon the first signs of what had been a large Indian encampment.

They drew up at the end of a long, double line of lodges. Only the circular marks were left in the dirt now. They were several days old. Dismounting, they walked past the blackened spots where fires had burned. There were drying skeletons of cattle which had been butchered and stripped. Buzzards hopped clumsily over the remains and rose reluctantly at their approach. As they moved, Sul stooped now and then to pick up a feather or a small object from the ground. By the time they had reached the end of the encampment he had half a dozen things in his hand. He stood, kicking thoughtfully at the charred sticks of a long dead fire. They extended from their center like spokes of a wheel.

"No one but a Cheyenne builds a fire just like that." He handed a worn moccasin to Pop. "Kiowa." The other items he dropped one by one. "That beaded porcupine quill is a Shoshone ornament, the beads are Mescalero Apache." He looked at Pop quizzically. "What would you say, old man, if you saw a wildcat, a bear, a panther and a fox hunting together?"

"I'd stop drinking." Pop's reply was emphatic.

Sul nodded gravely. "So, what would you do if you saw Apaches, Cheyennes, Kiowas, Arapahoes, Shoshone and Comanche riding together?"

"I'd yell for help." Pop was serious.

"That's what I'm going to do. They'll take the report at Fort Clark as they always do and file it away for channels. If there is anything the Army loves it is a channel which," he grinned, "is something through which you put something." He set his foot into the stirrup. "Let's ride."

The sun was two-thirds over on its course when the first, hazy blue smudges of the trees and buildings of San Sebastian were stained against the sky. Here the land rolled in gentle swells. Over the tumbling expanse, cattle grazed in small groups, dotting the landscape for miles. The three men saw no human sign until they topped a brush-studded rise and started down. Then, seeming to rise from the ground itself, a half-dozen horsemen moved

swiftly to flank them with silent convoy. They rode as
though they were unaware of the Rangers' presence although only a few yards separated them.

"Buenos dìas," Sul called.

"Buenos dìas, señor."

The greeting was echoed by only one of the men. He
was a lean Mexican in his early twenties. He rode with an
easy pride. His saddle was heavily encrusted with chased-
silver decoration. The broad, peaked sombrero he wore
with a knotted cord beneath his chin was ringed at the
brim with tiny, silver hawk's bells which tinkled with the
movement of the horse. No smile accompanied the gravely
courteous salute. He did no more than glance at the
Rangers, then turned his eyes ahead. For all the appearance of indifference, the implication that this was a chance
meeting, it was obvious that this was an escort, well armed
and suspicious. No further words were exchanged and the
San Sebastian riders kept their distance with military precision, pacing their mounts to meet that of the strangers.

As they drew nearer to the main ranch house, they
could make out the figures of mounted men and standing
spectators along what seemed to be a straight racing
course. Excited shouts came faintly to their ears.

The main house of the estancia followed the familar
design of the country, an open square with a broad patio
in the center. The windows were narrow and set high in
the adobe walls. Beyond, on both sides, stretched a series
of smaller buildings and a corral. A few blackjack oaks
and cottonwoods threw a lacy pattern of shade over the
main house, and all about them the ground seemed to
spring to colorful life with a profusion of phlox.

Sul reined up. Pop and Yancey drew to a halt beside
him and their escort abruptly checked their mounts.

Stretched in a double line, forming a lane of perhaps a
hundred yards, were rows of stakes the height of a
mounted man. On each was fastened a yellow, pumpkin-
like gourd. As they watched, one of the mounted men
wheeled out of the ranks, drove his spurs into his horse
and galloped to the far end of the line. Then, under whip
and spur, he sent the animal racing down between the

rows of stakes. A bright-bladed machete, fastened to the rider's wrist by a leather thong, whistled and flashed in the sunlight. At full speed, swaying from side to side with perfect rhythm, the rider drove at a thundering pace. He whirled the machete from left to right, right to left like a sabre. There was a steady plopping sound as the blade sheared through the gourds, cutting them in half. At the end of the run, wheeling abruptly, he pulled his horse into a rearing salute.

"Olé! Olé!" The shouts of the spectators rose.

Pirouetting before Anna De Lacey, who was watching from horseback, the rider swept his sombrero off with a theatrical gesture. Then, simultaneously everyone became aware of the presence of strangers. The cheers died and there was an air of wary tension. Anna De Lacey shaded her eyes with a hand and then moved her mount from the crowd, advancing slowly toward the Rangers. Every eye was turned to follow her.

For a moment, there was astonishment in her expression and then she smiled with genuine pleasure. "Captain Carter," she called.

The Rangers walked their horses to meet her. She pushed the flat, low-crowned hat back and allowed it to dangle by the cord. Her eyes were bright as they traveled from Sul to Yancey to Pop.

"*Bienvenidos, amigos.* I did not hope that we would meet again so soon. Welcome to San Sebastian." She inclined her head with a silent question toward Pop.

"Ranger Warner, Ma'm." Sul made the introduction.

"I am happy to see all of you." She included Yancey with a special smile. "What brings you to San Sebastian?"

"We are on our way to Fort Clark and thought you might put us up for the night," Sul answered.

"But of course. My house is yours. Guests are rare and doubly welcome."

They were ringed now at a respectful distance by the people of San Sebastian who, taking their cue from the friendly tone of the *patrona,* stared curiously at the strangers and whispered to each other in muted excitement. Yancey looked at her with unconcealed pleasure.

She made a picture of youthful beauty in the short jacket and divided skirt of doeskin that had been tanned to the softness of sheer fabric. He marveled that the sun had left no mark on her clean, clear complexion.

"And my dancing Ranger." She moved to extend her hand to Yancey who took it clumsily. "Do you still enjoy the life in Texas?"

"Let's just say I'm getting used to it, Ma'm." He smiled at her.

They followed her as she walked her horse back toward the house. A young Indio was already fastening a fresh supply of gourds to the stakes and a new contestant was preparing for the run.

"As you see," she indicated the course, "we amuse ourselves with simple pleasures."

"Such as lopping off heads?" Sul's friendly grin robbed the question of any bite.

"Yes." She was serious. "I suppose that is what it really means although I had not thought of it in that way before. It is a game my vaqueros invented. They seem to enjoy it more when I watch. It is, as you suggest, a primitive sport."

They waited until the new rider completed his run, missing two of the gourds, and then moved as a body toward the house. A barefooted peon came running to take their horses. Anna led them to the shade of the portal.

"What may I offer you—food, drink or both?" A serving girl appeared without summons and stood waiting.

"A chance to wash up, Ma'm," Sul suggested.

"But of course." She spoke to the girl rapidly in Spanish and then turned to them. "Anita will show you to your rooms. Join me here later. It is, as you know, *Cinco de Mayo,* and for the holiday we have made some small preparations for the evening. Your presence will add to our pleasure." Her expression clouded. "Is it trouble that takes you to Fort Clark, Captain?"

"There's always trouble of one sort or another, Ma'm." Sul was noncommittal. "It's endemic in Texas."

"I see." She smiled vaguely.

Watching and listening to her, Yancey wondered if she knew of the uprising brewing along the border. If her relationship with Corbel was what the word "protector" suggested, such innocence didn't seem possible.

Her manner changed. "If there is to be more trouble," she added, "then we are indeed fortunate in having such men as the Rangers on our side." She nodded to the waiting girl and then addressed the men again. "*Hasta luego* and, if you wish, take advantage of a custom of the country—a siesta. I will see you later."

The girl led them to one wing of the house and opened the doors of three bedrooms as they went down the long corridor. Later, men servants brought hot water in large *ollas,* filling the portable zinc tubs until they almost overflowed. Piles of thick, fluffy towels were piled on a low stool.

It had been a long time since Yancey had experienced the luxury of a hot tub and he immersed himself contentedly, his knees protruding from the water as he tried to fit his length into the short tub. The steam rose in a cloud about him, made fragrant from the delicately scented soap in the water.

Later, he shaved carefully, wishing he had a change of clothing. He examined the rough jeans, the dusty boots and travel-stained shirt, thinking they weren't much in which to visit a lady. With a damp towel, he sponged them off as best he could, slicked down his hair and left the room with a feeling of excitement.

The staircase from the upper gallery ran on both sides to the patio. Yancey paused on the landing, looking down into the sun-mottled square. Anna De Lacey was seated in a high-backed wicker chair, shaped to the design of an outspread peacock's tail. In her hands she held a small embroidery hoop, but her fingers were idle. A kitten played about her feet, chasing a dried leaf. At the sound of Yancey's step she turned, tilting back her head and smiling.

"So soon?" she asked. "I thought, perhaps, a siesta after a long ride."

"I can always sleep." He grinned. "At least, that's what

I like to think. Talking with a pretty girl is another thing. That doesn't happen very often." He sat on the edge of a table and regarded her with undisguised admiration.

"And do you miss them, the pretty girls and all the other things you once took for granted?"

"It's a funny thing," he mused. "But, I guess I don't, really. After awhile you forget there are such things as girls—the kind you're used to, anyway."

"That would seem to me to be an extremely unhappy confession. It is such a strange, almost savage existence you lead so far away from home."

"And what about you?"

She inclined her head. "Yes." The word was whispered. "For me, also, it is an unnatural way of life and not at all what I was trained for. So," her eyes met his with a wistful smile, "we are both strangers in a strange land, is it not so?" She rose and smoothed out the flowing skirt. "It is a pleasant time of the afternoon. Would you care to walk with me for a while?"

As they walked, Yancey took in the details of the establishment. San Sebastian was self-sufficient. In a row of small, adobe buildings there were a harness shop, blacksmith, a wagonwright, and storehouses; even a little *tienda,* or store, at which the people of the ranch could purchase tobacco and articles of clothing. Quarters for those employed were scattered haphazardly. Small children played in the dirt and old men were drowsy in the late sun, leaning against still-warm walls and smoking endlessly. There was a muted rhythm of community life about the scene.

At a heavy pole driven solidly into the ground, two men hoisted a squealing pig into the air by its hind legs and deftly slit its throat. The rich, dark blood cascaded into a pan on the ground and at the sight of it Yancey felt his stomach turn. He looked quickly at Anna De Lacey but she gave the spectacle only a passing glance. He frowned mentally. Most girls would have turned away in horror, real or simulated, from the sight.

Not until they were well past the buildings did she

speak, and then there was a small tone of amusement in her voice.

"You were shocked, were you not? I could see it in your face. You thought, What sort of a woman is this, when I displayed none of the conventional dismay at the slaughtering of a hog." She shrugged. "It is a necessary operation and I have come to accept it as such."

"I can't figure you out," he confessed.

"Why should you try? It is much simpler to take things as they are. I see you mentally measuring me by the standards of the girls you knew in Virginia. You say to yourself, What sort of a person is this Anna De Lacey?" Her smile was wistful. "I'll tell you, my friend. She is not so much different than those you have known. I live here in what is, almost, a man's world. There are women on the estancia, of course, but the vaqueros and my peones regard them as little more than instruments for breeding or pleasure. So, I, who am unique here, must preserve a detachment. Would you have me a helpless, trembling female constantly seeking shelter behind her sex?"

"No," he replied slowly, "I guess I'd have you just the way you are."

"I survive through the most elementary of processes. The cattle mate and reproduce themselves. I sell them. Simple, *verdad?*"

He nodded without comment. They walked, seemingly without destination. Behind them, in the purpling hush of a swift twilight, the buildings of the estancia seemed to draw closer together against the approach of night. She glanced at the cloudless, salmon-colored sky and sighed.

"It is a melancholy time of day, is it not? The sun not actually gone, the darkness just beyond the horizon. When my husband was alive, we had a winter home in Cuernavaca, near Mexico City. For just a few seconds, at an hour such as this, the snow-capped peaks of the volcanoes would appear as giant mounds of strawberry mousse. For some reason it always made me sad, perhaps because the beauty was so fleeting."

It was the first time she had ever mentioned her husband in his presence or suggested that she had known a life different from the one she now led. He wondered why.

As though sensing the unasked question she shook her head with a brief smile of apology. "I am moody." The confession came regretfully. "The *dolor* seems to grow upon me of late. I try looking ahead into the years to come and can see nothing."

"Why do you stay here then?" The question was a natural one.

"Where would I go?" Her slim shoulders shrugged indifferently. "No, that isn't right. Why, is the question. Why and to what purpose? My life, as I knew it, is like your nursery rhyme, Humpty-Dumpty. It cannot be put together again." She turned to look at him with an engaging smile. "Enough about me. Do you not remain along this part of the border for an unusually long time? I understood that your headquarters were to the north."

Yancey couldn't help but wonder if she was making idle talk or seeking information for Corbel about the movements of the Rangers.

"Sul," he said after a moment, "makes his headquarters where he spreads his blanket. There is a lot of territory to cover and only a few men to do the job. No one ever asks Sul why he does something. They only ask where or when."

"You make him sound formidable."

"I guess that's the word for Sul. Formidable." He nodded. "He gets ten feet tall at times."

They came to the edge of a dry creek bed. The stones lay bleached and bone-white. The cottonwoods, once nourished by the creek, were skeletal and tangled. A hawk came to rest silently on a withered limb on the opposite bank. Its head turned slowly to search the ground for an unwary lizard that would provide a supper. Mechanically, Yancey looked around for a stone to shy at it. Nearby, at the edge of a thorny patch of chaparral, lay a polished rock. He bent and reached for it. The sound was one he had heard so many times that in that fatal second it did not register. He saw the triangular head reared in anger, the rattles vibrating in fury and felt the sharp, needle-like pain of the strike. With a yell, he jerked his hand away, staring at it stupidly. The sound halted abruptly and the rattlesnake glided away before he could stamp it with his heavy boots.

With a short scream, Anna De Lacey snatched his wrist, twisting the hand to see the twin punctures, turning slightly blue now. She ripped the colored scarf from about her neck and bound it tightly over the veins within the elbow's crook.

"Your knife, hurry!" She gestured at his belt. "I have seen this happen to my men. There is little time."

Still staring dumbly at his hand, Yancey drew the blade from its sheath, hesitating with the point resting lightly where the fangs had entered.

She snatched it from him and with a steady hand made a cross cut. The knife which he had honed so carefully to a razor sharpness made a faintly rasping sound as the skin parted. Blood welled suddenly. With a shudder, Anna lifted the hand to her mouth but Yancey pulled it away and put it to his lips. He sucked the warm, sweetish flow and spat. Already he could feel the numbness gather in his arm and felt a throbbing where the tourniquet held back the natural flow of blood. He still had not fully grasped what had happened.

"Sit down." She pushed at him. "Wait here. Don't move any more than is necessary. Exertion only hastens the poison through your body." Then she was gone, running toward the house, the full skirt whipping high to her knees.

Alone, Yancey experienced a curious feeling of detachment. He tried to follow the syndrome of the poisoning. There was the throbbing numbness in his arm and a feeling of nausea. Then came a sharp, shooting pain and a sense of constriction in his chest. He felt an unnatural heat begin to generate in his body and this was followed by an odd lassitude. He found himself wondering how long it took the venom to reach the heart and paralyze its muscles. He had heard that the tourniquet should be loosed at intervals to allow a small amount of the poison to circulate. He tried to work the knot of the scarf with his fingers but discovered they were inept. He gave up finally, dropping his head between bowed shoulders. He began to vomit uncontrollably.

They took him back to the house, stretched on blankets on the flat bed of a wagon. He was only dimly aware of the motion and of the anxious faces of Sul and Pop. When he tried to look at them he was unable to focus his eyes. He attempted to speak and his lips trembled soundlessly.

"Don't try to talk. Take it easy. You're going to be all right." Sul made no effort to hide his concern.

Sometime during the night he awoke to find Sul, Pop and Anna De Lacey seated about his bed. The girl reached over, wrung out a piece of toweling in a basin and wiped the sticky perspiration from his face. He smiled weakly and his eyes, unaccountably heavy, closed again.

In the morning he awoke, a little astonished to discover he was still alive. He tried to sit up, found he was too weak and slumped heavily back into the pillows where he lay, staring at the ceiling. The pain no longer wracked him but the nausea persisted.

His head turned and he saw Sul, back to the bed, staring out the window. Nearby was a chair, and on the floor beside it, a saucer with a mound of cigarette butts.

"You been here all night?" The words were half-whispered and wryly disbelieving.

Sul turned quickly and came to the bedside. "How are you feeling?"

"I feel like hell, if you really want to know." He paused, taking a deep breath. "I guess I'm pretty stupid, Sul."

"Careless, maybe. But never mind about that as long as you're all right. It was sort of touch and go for a while. You were out of your head. Madame De Lacey was here most of the night. You had us real worried."

"I guess she saved my life," Yancey confessed. "I forgot everything I'd ever heard about what to do with a snake bite. I guess I'd better get up." He again tried to raise his shoulders but Sul pushed him back gently.

"You stay where you are." Sul hesitated. "I'm going to leave you here. Pop and I will go on to Clark. I have a feeling there isn't a lot of time. We'll swing back this way in two or three days and pick you up."

"I'm all right," Yancey protested. "Let me get on my feet for a few minutes."

"Don't be a fool." Sul's words were sharp. "You're in no shape to ride. A few hours in that sun and you'd be as sick as a poisoned hog. I know what I'm talking about."

There was a tap at the door and Anna De Lacey came in. She looked first at the figure on the bed and then at Sul.

"How is he feeling?" She crossed quickly to touch her fingers to Yancey's forehead. They were cool and soft. "No fever," she said and smiled at him.

"I'll be fine if I can get out of this bed." Yancey felt ridiculously helpless.

"I'd like to leave him here, Ma'm." Sul ignored Yancey's protestation. "I don't think he's in any shape to travel. If it's all right with you?"

"Of course it's all right, Captain." Her eyes brightened. "Or were you suggesting I would be compromised by having a man in my house?"

"No, Ma'm," Sul drawled. I just don't like to put you to any trouble. We'll be back this way in a few days."

"I assure you I will welcome the company." She turned to Yancey. "Would you eat some breakfast?"

Yancey shook his head. On the point of assuring them that he was fit to travel, he changed his mind. Only a real big fool, he told himself, would argue about staying here with a girl like Anna De Lacey.

She nodded and turned away. "I'll send up some cool melon. Later, when you feel like it, we'll try a couple of eggs." She seemed briskly efficient. "Will you join me for coffee, Captain, or would you rather I had it sent to you here?"

"I'll be down directly, Ma'm." Sul waited until she closed the door behind her and then turned to Yancey. "Maybe it's a good thing this happened. I'd like to know a little more about San Sebastian. You just hang around, court the *patrona* and keep your eyes open. If anything should happen and I don't get back, then you make it into

Brownsville and hang around until someone shows up or find your way to Willow Bend on the river. Take care of yourself." His heavy hand touched Yancey's shoulder with brief affection and then he was gone, closing the door softly behind him.

Chapter Eleven

In Matamoros the *Jefe de Policia* leaned back in his chair, feet cocked indolently on a scarred table. Idly, he spun the cylinder of a revolver and the sound was a soft, sinister chatter. His eyes never left the faces of Park Manning and Dewey who stood uneasily before him.

"I dislike repeating myself." He spoke quietly in accented English. "What are you doing in Matamoros?"

"For the past three days we've been in that stinking hole you call a jail." Park attempted to inject a note of outraged innocence in his voice.

The chief of police, in the uniform of a captain in the Mexican Army, nodded agreeably. "We are a poor but hospitable country. Our accommodations are without certain comforts. However, the cell is yours for as long as you care to occupy it. Why are you in Matamoros?"

"Listen, Chief," Park was earnestly aggrieved. "This town is full of Americans. What makes us so special? How come we get picked up and tossed into the hoosegow without a charge? Nobody has even said what we did."

The Mexican put the empty revolver down on the table, leaned farther back and stared at the ceiling reflectively. "Why indeed." The question seemed to please him. "As for a charge?" he mused. "We have a book filled with statutes. It is quite possible that you have violated one or more of them. My police force is small but efficient." The smile was brilliant.

"Well, name it then!" Dewey exploded, ignoring Park's

warning glance. "Give a name to what we've done an' let us begin servin' our time or work out a fine." He glared at the young officer.

Sensing, somehow, that Park represented the authority, the captain ignored Dewey's outburst. He continued an interested scrutiny of a crack in the ceiling. After a moment, Park spoke apologetically.

"To tell the truth, Captain," he said, "we got into a little trouble in Brownsville and decided to take a trip into Mexico for our health."

"What was the nature of your trouble?" The officer didn't seem to be particularly interested.

"It was just sort of shootin' trouble, Captain." Manning ventured the information dejectedly.

"My country is honored that you decided to transfer your talents." The feet dropped to the floor with a thump and the man glared at them. "The scum of Texas washes constantly against our shore."

"Now, Captain." Park was amused. "We get some bad Mexicans across the river too. It's about an equal division, I'd say. Sort of give and take."

The officer's intelligent face lighted with a brief smile. "Perhaps," he agreed. "I will tell you why you were taken into custody. It was because you did nothing." He smiled at their blank expressions. "That, in itself, is unusual. Here, in Matamoros you did not get drunk, as is the custom of your countrymen. You have displayed a politeness to the townspeople. You have avoided fights and gave no provocation for any brawls which occur nightly in the cantinas. You lived quietly in a room in the *posada* by the river. Let me tell you, this behavior is so unusual that I became suspicious. I say, What are they doing here? What do they want? What are they looking for? Now, you tell me." The final words were whiplashed.

"Well, I'll just be dogged-damned!" Dewey's astonishment was genuine. "This is the first time I have ever heard of a man getting arrested for minding his own business an' that's a fact."

"Honest, Captain," Park interposed, "it's like I said. We kept out of trouble here because we already got enough trouble across the river to last us a spell. We figured to be quiet and mind our own business."

"Those are admirable traits but so unusual in border towns as to excite suspicion." He was silent for a moment. "How well do you know the border on your side of the river?" He said finally.

"We've traveled most of it from Brownsville to Eagle Rock," Manning admitted and then added ingeniously: "Usually we were travelin' fast, a jump or two ahead of the Rangers, so we didn't have much time to take in the scenery, if that's what you mean. However, I'd say we know it real well."

"I have a friend," the Captain spoke slowly, "who has need of men who are familiar with the border—the fording places, the routine movements of the Rangers, the towns where a few dollars in the right hands would prevent the curious from asking questions. Such men would be paid well."

"It begins to sound real interestin', Captain," Park ventured cautiously. "Particularly the pay part."

"The work I have in mind involves a certain element of danger."

"Just livin' along the border involves that, Captain." Manning shrugged indifferently.

"Can you handle teams and heavy wagons?" the Mexican asked.

"Anything that'll roll we can drive." Dewey grinned.

The officer opened a drawer and drew out their belts and holsters, shoving them across the table. "You may have your guns back. If you are looking for a temporary occupation, I will speak to my friend when I see him. It is possible something may be arranged. If you stay in Matamoros you will remain at the *posada* so I will know where to find you." It was an order.

"We're pretty comfortable there." Manning nodded his understanding.

"Bueno! I will send word to you if and when my friend desires a meeting." He leaned back against the wall again, whistling softly, terminating the interview without additional words.

Outside, Park and Dewey walked along the pocked street toward the river.

"That's a funny one," Dewey remarked. "Why us?"

"Because you have a dishonest face, I guess." Park was occupied with his own thoughts. "If this is what I think it is, we may be on to something. The problem is to keep alive. Too many characters out of Texas on this side know us. That's the real danger. So, we keep to ourselves like we've been doing, only more so."

The week they had spent in the little town across the river from Brownsville had confirmed their suspicions as to the extent of the traffic in stolen cattle. Day after day, they had seen small herds, stringy from hard driving, pound through the roads to be loaded onto lighters along the bank and later ferried to waiting ships. Idling along the shore, they had counted a dozen different Texas brands. Between ships, cattle by the hundreds bawled and milled about in huge pens under the watchful eyes of tough, bearded men.

"I'm surprised that there's a piece of beefsteak left in Texas." Manning had whistled his astonishment.

Once, pretending a drunken drowsiness, they had propped themselves against the warm, adobe wall of a cantina and watched as two covered wagons lumbered up the small rise. A sudden gust of wind had caught at the canvas, ballooning it out, and they had a brief glance at what could only be wooden rifle cases and small, ten-pound kegs in which powder was usually carried.

"What I'd like to know," Park said to Dewey later, "is where those wagons go when they leave here. If what Sul heard was true, the Indians aren't getting them yet. So, they must be unloading and stockpiling in a depot somewhere. The day old Iron Shirt gets his hands on them is the day I'd like to be someplace away from Texas."

Walking now toward the river and the small inn where they occupied a scantily furnished room, they avoided the bars and ignored the soft greetings of girls standing in doorways or half-leaning from windows. This was a tough and boisterous community where trouble exploded with a sudden, senseless fury. Street brawls were so common that no one paid any attention to them. The fights flared quickly and with little more cause than a careless word. They ended when one of the contestants lay bleeding or unconscious or, more frequently, dead. Eventually, a couple of dirty soldiers came to drag the vanquished away with as little ceremony as the dead bull is hauled from the plaza on the day of a corrida. Ordinarily, the rowdy atmosphere of the place would have delighted Park and Dewey, for they led lonely lives for the most part. They would have stood shoulder to shoulder in the largest and noisiest of the cantinas, reveling in the sound and sights. Now, however, they kept to themselves, taking their meals at the inn, spending the hours in between in their room.

"Dogged if I wouldn't like to stop in for a drink." Dewey sniffed hungrily at the acrid aroma of tequila, beer and raw whiskey as it floated through the open door of a cantina. "I'd like to drink me a drink and twirl me a girl." He looked hopefully at Manning.

"And have someone recognize you and everyone in town know that a couple of Rangers had come across the river. I can't think of a quicker way to get into trouble." Park shook his head. "We may be on to something with the Mexican Captain. So, we'll just play it quiet and wait for him to make a move." He grinned suddenly. "I forgot to ask. Can you really handle a team and wagon so'd you'd look an' act like a driver?"

"I can hold the reins," Dewey admitted. "I guess that's about all there is to it."

Chapter Twelve

At Fort Clark, Sul sat in Major Wakefield's office, experiencing the helplessness he always felt when confronted by the military mind. He had told the officer in detail of the meeting between Corbel and Iron Shirt and

of the irrefutable signs of an Indian rebellion. Major
Wakefield had been soberly interested. He was a man with
long experience and knew as well as Sul what would
happen if the Indians, fully armed and supplied, went on
the war path.

"I believe everything you have told me, Captain Carter." Wakefield was grave. "But I'm damned if I know
what we can do about it."

"One thing you can't do, Major." Sul was drawn and
weary from hard days in the saddle. "You can't wait until
the trouble starts."

"Unfortunately, that's the way the Army has to oper-
ate." Wakefield shook his head. "I can't touch Corbel in
Mexico. I can't even put a hand on him when he comes
into Texas. For all we're supposed to know, he is a
general in the Mexican Army, nothing more. Can you
imagine what would happen to me if I arrested him on the
vague charge that he planned to supply arms to the Indians for a general uprising?"

"You could patrol the likely fording spots at the river."
Even as he made the suggestion Sul knew how thin it was.
"Or you can do what I've already done. Send some agents
into Mexico to track the munitions. This isn't going to be
just a few rifles but, maybe, a dozen or more wagons. Oh,
I know the objection. A dozen wagons cross, one at a
time, at a dozen different places." A rueful smile touched
his mouth. I guess I was just hoping you'd pull a rabbit
out of your hat."

"Rabbits, Captain," Wakefield smiled without humor,
"are getting scarcer every year."

"I'd take that to mean I'm on my own?"

"I'm afraid so."

"But after the Indians have the guns and a general
uprising is underway with towns burned and settlers mas-
sacred, the Army will step in to take appropriate mea-
sures? Is that it?" He slumped deep on his spine in the
chair, eying the Major angrily.

"I think we'd better have a drink." Wakefield reached
into a rough, board cabinet and withdrew a bottle of rye
whiskey. "I know enough about you, Captain, to under-

stand that there was nothing personal in that remark. The Army moves within certain, definitely restricted lines. They are as fixed and immutable as the stars."

The whiskey made a small, warm ball in Sul's stomach. After a moment, he relaxed, feeling some of the resentment drain from him. He really hadn't expected much more than a sympathetic ear.

"We can put you up for the night or as long as you care to stay." Wakefield pushed the bottle across the table with a silent invitation.

"We'll be on our way in the morning, Major. I'd like a bed now for twelve hours or so. Or," he amended, "at least until mess time. Whew! On an empty stomach that whiskey hits you."

Lying on a cot in the officers' quarters, Sul was dimly aware of the post's orderly activity and then he slept, the heavy, dreamless sleep of a thoroughly tired man.

Chapter Thirteen

The candles raised small cones of amber-colored light that spread in a wavering pool across the polished surface of the piano and rested softly on Anna De Lacey's cheek as she played a Chopin waltz. She turned once to smile at Yancey who watched her from the depths of a huge chair, half-obscured in the shadows.

It was difficult to realize that he was not in a familiar drawing room back in Virginia; that outside, the great prairie spread to the horizon where no light of rancher or homesteader glowed, that a vast loneliness surrounded them. On a small table within arm's reach was a cut-glass decanter of fine, French brandy and a box of rich Havana cigars. Sipping the brandy after dinner, rolling the cigar's fragrant smoke in his mouth, Yancey took a certain pleasure in the thought that what he drank and smoked were undoubtedly there for General Corbel.

"What do you brood upon?" He realized with a start that Anna had stop playing and, partly turned upon the low bench, was regarding him with a quizzical smile.

"I wasn't brooding; just thinking that this wasn't included in the list of inducements offered for enlistment in the Rangers. Austin is missing a persuasive argument."

She rose lightly, took a cigarette from a thin case and bent toward a candle's flame.

"Of course," he continued with a grin, "if you have to get bitten by a rattlesnake to enjoy it, I'd imagine that would rob it of some attractiveness."

"It has been pleasant having you here. I am alone too much." She leaned against the piano and Yancey was certain she knew the picture she created. "Also," she laughed and the sound rippled gently, "you are a little astonished by me and that is always entertaining. I don't quite fit into the categories you have for those who are ladies and those who are not. You wonder if you could make love to me and whether you should try."

Yancey squirmed. She was too smart. Probably a good many girls would have thought the same thing only they wouldn't have said it. It put a man off balance.

"I am not offended. On the contrary, I think I should be piqued if the thought had not crossed your mind. Come." She extended her hand. "Let us walk outside for a while."

He came out of the chair quickly and her hand rested lightly on his arm. The broad doors opened on the patio, heavy with mimosa and the deep, grapelike flowering of the jacaranda. Somewhere in the distance, a voice sang to the accompaniment of a guitar.

"I often wonder what the Mexican songwriters would do without *dolor* and *corazon*. Sadness and heart. All of their music is built around those two words." Her mood changed abruptly. "Where do you go when you leave San Sebastian?"

"I've got a rendezvous with Sul." He checked himself,

nagged again by the small suspicion that she was seeking information.

She seemed not to notice the hesitation. "Isn't it curious how that word, a French word, has crept into the speech of this southwest where Spanish is so common. I have heard it used many times by men who, I am certain, have not the slightest idea it is foreign."

They crossed the flagstone patio to where a wide, oaken door, reinforced by iron straps and a heavy bolt, opened to the outside. Yancey slid back the bolt and pulled on a metal ring. The door swung inward without a sound and they stepped outside.

As always, the immensity of this land at night impressed itself upon him with an almost terrifying impact. He had not become accustomed to it. Back home, he thought, it would be cut up by neat farms and fields, broken by manor and cabin, cut into squares and rectangles by weathered railed fences, dotted by pasture and meadow. Here it was only a great cavern of silence.

Her hand tightened upon his arm and she pressed closer to him. "You feel it also, do you not?" Her voice was muted although there was no need to be quiet. "It still frightens me, even after so long a time."

Her face was lifted, soft and fragrant as a magnolia. Drawn irresistibly, although there was no invitation in her eyes, he bent and kissed her, not abruptly but gently, almost sadly. For a moment, she half-turned and he felt her warmth, the soft questing of her mouth and then she drew away with a small sigh.

"It has been a long time," she spoke softly, "since I have been kissed with gentleness."

In the distance, a dog barked suddenly. Having sounded the alarm the animal became silent.

At first, it seemed to be nothing more than a firefly, a tiny, dancing light that came and vanished. In the stillness, they heard the sound of small sticks breaking. Then, the light became steadier and more distinct. Mounted men moved out from the darkness, surrounding them. Yancey counted at least a dozen, rifles resting across their saddles, as they moved at a slow canter toward the approaching light.

"Do you keep a guard up all night?" He was surprised.

"It is the price of survival out here." She gazed at the dancing flicker and then she relaxed. "It is Andre." Her hand dropped away from his arm.

The coach, a lantern hanging beneath it, was a magnificent affair, heavily sprung, varnished and rubbed to a soft patina. Silver ornamentation curled in a complex design about the doors, ending in elaborate handles. As it drew to a halt, a groom, riding beside the driver, leaped down to swing the door open and Yancey had a glimpse of the heavy brocaded upholstery.

General Andre Corbel stepped down with surprising lightness for so heavy a frame. His glance flicked over Yancey without recognition or expression and then moved on to Anna De Lacey.

"You must forgive the hour, Madame." Corbel bowed stiffly. "And the intrusion on your hospitality. We were delayed on the road by a broken wheel."

"General Corbel." Anna extended a slim hand with a warm smile. "Old friends can never intrude." She paused for just a second. "You have already met Ranger Carter at Don Porfirio's."

"Of course. Forgive me. The light is bad and I did not recognize you." The smile was mechanical, never reaching the eyes. If Corbel thought Yancey's presence at San Sebastian strange, nothing in his manner betrayed the fact.

"Come inside. We will get you a drink and something to eat."

Yancey was puzzled by her use of the plural until he realized that she used it to refer to herself. It tickled him a little, also, that Anna did not do the obvious thing and explain about the snake bite. For the moment, at least, Corbel was allowed to draw his own conclusions. Yancey wondered what he was thinking.

When they turned to re-enter the patio, Anna linked her arms with theirs. It was an easy, friendly gesture and they walked this way to the drawing room where a servant was already waiting. She curtseyed silently to the visitor.

Watching the man, Yancey waited for some sign of familiarity toward Anna but the general maintained the status of a casual and infrequent guest. Yancey thought he saw him glance quickly at the decanter and brandy glass beside the chair together with the half-consumed cigar.

In easy, fluent Spanish, Anna De Lacey gave the servant orders for food to be brought and then she selected a fresh glass and poured a brandy for Corbel and offered him a cigar from the humidor.

"Now!" She settled herself on a couch. "Tell us what brings you to San Sebastian."

A small shadow of a frown appeared on Corbel's face, lasting no more than a second. He stood, legs apart as though rooting himself to the carpet. He savored the brandy with appreciation and then dipped the end of his cigar in the liquor before putting down the glass and lighting the tobacco.

With unmistakable rudeness Corbel ignored the question, speaking instead to Yancey. "And how is your brother, the redoubtable Captain Carter?"

There was the smallest suggestion of sarcasm in the description of Sul which Yancey pretended not to hear.

"He's somewhere undoubtedly being, as you say, redoubtable."

A servant came in to set a table at one side of the room while two others brought in platters of cold meat and fowl together with chilies, beans and a small *casuela* of smoking stew. Without apology, Corbel seated himself, tucked a napkin beneath his chin and gave his full attention to the food. He washed it down with glasses of wine and belched contentedly, indifferent to the presence of others. Yancey glanced in Anna De Lacey's direction. She was occupied with a small hoop of embroidery, seemingly unaware of the gluttony. When Corbel had finished, he leaned back and lit a cigar.

Yancey was uncomfortable. He could sense a constraint in the room, of which he was the cause. He stood up.

"I am going to be on my way early in the morning, Madame De Lacey." He crossed to her. "Chances are I'll be gone before you are awake. Thank you for everything."

Anna put aside her needlework and arose. "It has been most pleasant having you here." She extended her hand with a smile. "I hope that it won't take another accident to make you our guest again. The gates of San Sebastian are always open to you."

Yancey released her hand and turned to Corbel. "Good night, General."

With deliberate rudeness Corbel remained seated. He waved a salute of parting with the cigar but offered no word. Yancey flushed with sudden anger, nodded briefly and turned on his heel.

In his room, undressing for bed, Yancey laughed with soft embarrassment to himself. Sure, Corbel had behaved badly but that wasn't what made him sore. It was the man's assumption of privilege at San Sebastian and the relationship with Anna De Lacey it implied. You're jealous, he told himself with some surprise. You're jealous over a girl you've only seen twice. It's a funny feeling, like being sick in your stomach.

For a long time, he lay sleepless. He listened to the low, humming sound of conversation and once he thought he heard Corbel's voice rise in anger, but he couldn't be sure. Anyhow, Corbel was a swine and a renegade. With this pleasant thought as a mild opiate he slept.

Chapter Fourteen

The rendezvous at Willow Bend was separated from Mexico by a hundred yards where the Rio Grande cut through the gently sloping banks. From where they were camped, restlessly awaiting the return of Sul, the Rangers could watch the men working in their scraggly fields. In the afternoons, young boys drove their herds of goats homeward. Now and then, women and girls came to the river to pound their wash against smooth rocks and the Rangers amused themselves by calling rude but good-natured invitations to a frolic. A girl would duck her head, smothering a laugh, but the older women sternly ignored the boisterous gringos. From somewhere a distant church bell tolled in the morning and afternoon. In the brief twilights, boys gathered on the opposite shore offering melons, papayas, chickens and strung chilies for sale. The Rangers met them in mid-stream to bargain over their produce. But, from these seemingly innocent encounters, reports of the Rangers' camp, their number, their movements filtered back to a *Jefe de Policia* in Matamoros and from there were relayed to a huge estancia halfway between the border town and Ciudad Monterrey in the interior.

The fortress-like structure of Andre Corbel reared starkly on the rolling land that was buttressed on the south by the first of the mountains. The thick walls of stone formed a hollow square within which dwelt a small community. Some of the rooms were no larger than prison cells, but the quarters of Corbel spread and rambled along one side with a lavish regard for the man's comfort. Furniture from Spain and Italy gleamed with dark perfection. Silks and porcelains from China, brought in through the distant port of Acapulco, lightened the somber atmosphere of the often windowless apartments. Within the court were blacksmith and wheelwright, saddle and harness maker. A large well with bucket and windlass was set within the middle of the square and around it the servant women gathered to draw their water and exchange their gossip as though they lived in their native *poblado*. On the high walls, narrow embrasures commanded the approaches on all sides. Here sentries stood throughout the days and nights, being changed with military precision.

It was here that Andre Corbel spun his dreams of empire. The Indians would take Texas and then he would take Texas from the Indians. It was to be his province, independent of both the United States and Mexico, ruled alone by Andre Corbel, Emperor. He did not think the scheme fantastic. The Americans, he was convinced, were exhausted and sick of fighting after their fratricidal war and would offer no more than token opposition. The government in Mexico City was occupied by its own internal problems, racked by the continual plots of revolution. No real obstacle to his ambition presented itself. Supplied and armed, the Indians under Iron Shirt would range and kill, spreading terror, confusion and desolation among the Texans and driving them from the land. When this was done he would deal with Iron Shirt through bribery or deception; it mattered not which.

The design in the fabric of this dream was spoiled for Corbel but not by thoughts of opposition from the United States Army. The small, undermanned forts would be overwhelmed and Washington would have no desire to send more troops. Of this he was convinced. What threatened his plans was that small corps of dedicated men, the Texas Rangers. Ordinarily, he would have laughed aside the possibility of real interference from such a limited number, but there was something in the character of these Rangers that bothered him. He searched his knowledge of history for a parallel and found it in faraway India. There, a couple of regiments of professional soldiers had held the country for the British Empire against overwhelming odds. Here, in Texas, it was the Rangers, and the Rangers alone, who maintained a semblance of order against the greatest aggregation of renegades, bandits, rustlers and vengeful Indians ever gathered in one state. The Rangers could smash Andre Corbel's dream simply by destroying the shipments of arms and ammunition before they ever reached the tribes Iron Shirt had gathered into an alliance. So, he told himself, he must outwit a handful of men. His desperate need at the moment was an agent, a spy within the Rangers who would keep him advised as to their disposition and numbers.

Sitting alone now, he frowned as he turned the problem over in his mind. A small possibility of a solution existed in the person of Anna De Lacey. It was obvious that young Carter was infatuated with her. It might be possible for Anna to gather small bits of information from him about the movements and numbers of the Rangers. But he dismissed this as a thin hope. Contact between Anna and Carter would be too infrequent and the girl, Corbel thought angrily, seemed stubbornly reluctant to play the role offered.

He stood up and began to pace the room. He had on his payroll the shiftless, untrustworthy American, Rale Latham. When the man had come to him with the information that his son had been accepted by the Rangers, Corbel had thought he saw an end to his difficulty. Young Latham would pass on the information he had to his father and Rale would give it to Corbel. Something had happened. Corbel wasn't quite sure what. Latham had come to him with the news that Sullivan Carter had hung his son.

Walking up and down the room with deliberate stride, Corbel ran over in his mind the things he already knew. Something had alerted the Rangers to the Rio Grande. Instead of a routine patrol, which would ordinarily have brought them to the river and then back again to their headquarters at Davis, they were remaining. Then, an Indian runner from Fort Clark had brought him the news of Sullivan Carter's visit to the commanding officer there. What they had talked about and decided he could not know, but Carter's presence at the post was out of normal procedure. Also, the small group on the American side of the river were obviously awaiting orders or reinforcements. He knew each small detail of their lives in camp. Ordinarily, with time on their hands, they would have gone into nearby Brownsville in search of amusement. Instead, they had developed a routine pattern. By day, only two or three remained at the bend of the river. The others drifted away, up and down stream, keeping a watch on the most obvious fording places. By night, one was always on watch at these spots.

Time was pushing Corbel into a corner and he knew it. Iron Shirt was growing more suspicious and impatient over the delay in the delivery of the promised arms. How much longer would he wait? How much longer could he command the loyalty of the fiercely individual chiefs he had gathered into a loose confederation? Already, in Corbel's storerooms were sufficent stocks of guns and ammunition to supply Iron Shirt. Corbel's greed for more and more cattle had made him delay turning them over to the savages. Also, he must have double the supply—gun for gun, powder charge for powder charge—he would give the Indians in order to supply his own army when the time came to confront Iron Shirt with his duplicity. On an impulse, he rang for a servant and told him to send Rale Latham to him.

He had no real faith in Latham, but the man was one of the few Americans in his employ who was not wanted by the authorities in Texas. Therefore, he could go and come across the river border without fear. For a brief time, Latham appeared to render a real service when he reported that he hung Sullivan Carter from his own horse. This, though, had proved to be nothing more than another of the man's empty boasts. No one knew how Sullivan had escaped, but there was no denying the fact that he was alive.

Latham entered the room with an attempted swagger, implying that he met Corbel on equal terms. Corbel studied him coldly.

"I want Sullivan Carter to come across the river. What will bring him?"

Latham's eyes darted hopefully toward a table with its humidor of cigars and decanter of brandy. "I don't know for sure, General. If he was to get mad enough over something he'd come over alone to take on the whole Mexican Army."

"What would make him that angry?" Corbel seated himself but did not offer a chair to Latham.

"I don't rightly know," Latham confessed. "But," he added, "Sul Carter's mighty touchy. He's trigger-touchy but he's smart. It'd have to be something that didn't look at all like a trap."

Corbel relented and waved toward the table. "Help yourself to a drink."

Latham went eagerly across the room and poured himself a brimming glass of spirits. Corbel watched him absently. A small idea began to shape itself in his mind. Surprisingly enough, Latham voiced it for him.

"Sul sets a lot of store by that young brother of his." Latham's mind worked slowly. "If he was to get into trouble, say in Matamoros, where the Mexican police could hold him, I'd say Sul would come a-hellin' across the river to get him out. He wouldn't wait for anyone else to act. You just might get Sul Carter in your hip pocket that way."

Corbel blew softly between thick lips. A cantina brawl in Matamoros would be enough to have the policia hold the younger brother. News of this could easily be passed around Brownsville and eventually reach the Rangers at Willow Bend. Still, Corbel mused, it probably wasn't enough. Sullivan was a disciplinarian. If he believed that Yancey was in trouble with the Mexican authorities through a fault of his own, then he might well leave him in their hands to serve out his punishment. No, that way was leaving too much to chance.

"Bring young Carter to me here." Corbel voiced the command almost absently.

"How am I a-goin' to do that?" Latham was confused.

The General stood up as a signal of dismissal. "I don't know. Just do it and that will bring Captain Carter. I want to know where he is before we start the wagon drive." He nodded curtly and turned away.

For a moment Latham stood indecisively, staring at the inflexible back of his employer. Then, with a resigned shake of his head, he shuffled from the room.

Chapter Fifteen

          Sul and Pop were two days out of Fort Clark
on the return trip to Willow Bend. They had been driving
themselves hard and both they and the animals were
feeling the pace.

"We'd better lay over a night in Three Wells." Sul
wiped at his red-rimmed eyes. "The horses need a rest and
I need one from your cooking, if that's what you call it."

"I never got around to naming it." Pop was serious.
"Chef's delight is close enough, I guess."

As they entered the first reaches of the dusty main
street of Three Wells, they looked at each other, puzzled.
The scattered houses they passed seemed tightly shuttered
against the day. No children played in the bare yards, no
washing hung on the lines, no women came to stand in the
doorways to watch their passing, as was usual. Farther
into the town the desertion was more pronounced. Ordinarily, this was a busy community, a relay station for the
stage, a gathering place for those from outlying farms and
small ranches. Today, the street was empty. The board-
walks on both sides were stripped of the loungers who
followed the shade. The only sound came from the Buckhorn Saloon—the tinny, monotonous beat of a piano and
a sudden shout of drunken laughter.

They nudged their weary horses toward a hitching rail
before a square, adobe building over which the sheriff's
sign hung crookedly. Looping the reins in a loose tie, they
stood for a moment, staring about, and then Sul crossed
the loose boards and pushed open the door. The room was
dust-filled. By a battered table a chair lay overturned on
the floor. Old papers and circulars were scattered about
and two empty whiskey bottles had rolled into a corner.

Connecting with the front room was a single large cell. The barred door was open.

"It's not like Walt Decker to keep an office like this." Sul's eyes traveled over the bare walls and halted on a gun rack. It was empty. Ordinarily, there would have been a couple of rifles and a shotgun there on the pegs, oiled and carefully cared for.

Sul walked into the cell and lifted a coarse blanket from the thin mattress of corn shucks. There was a large, brown stain on the wool. When he bent it in his hands, a thin crust cracked and small, rustlike particles flaked into his hands. Dried blood.

"What do you suppose is going on here?" Sul turned again to Pop. "Walt wouldn't run a shop like this."

"It doesn't look as though anyone has been running it." Pop picked up one of the bottles and sniffed it. "Offhand, I'd say that the lawing business in Three Wells has struck a real low ebb."

Outside again, they swung up into their saddles and headed down the street toward a livery stable. As they passed the saloon, the faces of three men appeared above the half-doors and appraising eyes followed them with listless curiosity.

The stable doors were closed. Without dismounting, Sul slid a foot from the stirrup and kicked at the weathered doors. Finally, one-half swung open a few cautious inches and a man peered at them. Sudden relief flooded over his face, and he hastily made the opening large enough for them to ride in. Then he quickly threw a heavy, wooden bar down, locking them all inside.

"What the devil are you up to, Gil?" Sul leaned forward, staring into the upturned face. "What's going on around here, anyhow?"

"Am I sure glad to see you, Captain," Gilbert Martin sighed tiredly.

Sul and Pop dismounted. "Come on, man." Sul was impatient. "What are you afraid of? Where is everyone?"

"They're locked inside their houses like me, afraid to go out. The whole town is spooked."

"Of what?" Sul grasped the man's shoulder angrily. "Make some sense will you?"

"They took over the whole town. You wouldn't believe it could happen." The words came in a torrent. "At first they just seemed to be horsin' around, drinkin' an' carousin'. Then, all of a sudden they got mean, began to break things up, ridin' people down in the streets, takin' what they wanted from the stores. Walt Decker tried to put a stop to it an' they emptied their guns in him, all four of them pumpin' slugs into Walt's body an' laughin' like crazy while they're doin' it."

"Who took over the town?" Sul shook the trembling man.

"The leader's a fellow named Joe Morse. He's been in an' out of Three Wells before. He's got three with him, strangers. Like I say, they killed Walt first. Then they run Jesse Comber out of his saloon and when he tried to come back with a gun, they beat him somethin' awful an' dragged him up an' down the street at the end of a rope until there was nothin' but a few bloody bones left. They took that half-wit girl of Devlin's into the saloon an' no one seen her since. She's probably dead by now. You wouldn't believe it could happen."

"Do you mean to tell me that the people of Three Wells just stood for all this? Four men against a whole town?" Sul stared with amazement at the shaking man.

"Like I say, you just wouldn't believe it. They got some hangers-on in there with them now; the shiftless riffraff that never done an honest day's work in their lives. Mayor Porter tried to stand up to them. I'll say that for him. He went to the Buckhorn to try an' talk some sense. They stripped him buck naked an' run him down the length of the street an' back until he near died. I tell you they're crazy, just plain out of their heads with whiskey. Some of us figured that when they drank up everything they'd maybe move on. We bin just waitin' an' hopin' for them to get their fill an' quit. We figured that when the stage come we could get word to the outside for help but it ain't due until next week. By that time if they're still here there ain't goin' to be nothin' left of Three Wells. How many Rangers you got with you, Captain?"

"Enough," Sul clipped the word. He glanced at Pop who slid a rifle from his saddle scabbard. "Take care of the horses. Wipe them down good and feed them well."

"You goin' in there alone, Captain?" Martin voiced his disbelief. "They'll gut you."

"I'm sure not going to stand here and wait for the stage." He turned to Pop. "I'll take a little walk."

The old man nodded almost absently. They had ridden together for so long that further words were unnecessary. Pop knew where Sul was going and Sul knew where Pop would be.

The dust erupted in tiny spurts from beneath his boots as Sul crossed the street. He wasn't happy with the odds. There was a good chance that this could be the last walk he would ever take. Someone had to do it and this was what the state of Texas paid him for. It was hard to figure; a whole town losing its nerve. He headed directly for the saloon and pushed through the latticed doors without hesitation.

For a second after he entered, there was complete silence in the room. The noisy talk halted. A couple of drunks lifted soggy faces and stared vacantly at him. Four men in a stud game halted their play, shifting in their chairs to watch as he went to the bar. Then the dealer, a huge, bearded man, undoubtedly their leader, began flipping single cards to the other players. His gaze still on Sul, he laughed suddenly, harshly. Broad grins spread across several faces.

Sul wore no badge of office. He stood at the bar while the man behind it stared at him with a gleam of anticipation in his eyes.

"Whiskey." Sul made the request casual.

The bartender hesitated, glanced furtively at the card table and then, with a sudden whinnying laugh, set a half-filled bottle and a glass out.

Sul poured a drink slowly and drank it, his gaze on the expectant men reflected in the mirror behind the bar.

"That'll be two dollars," the bartender snickered, revealing a mouthful of broken and yellowed teeth.

Without a change of expression Sul dropped two silver dollars on the counter. He drank his whiskey slowly, half of his body canted against the bar.

"The second drink'll be four dollars, stranger." Again the bartender snickered and shot a glance for approval at the card table.

"Get out." Sul's eyes lifted but his voiced remained soft. He could feel the tension in the room now, a surprised wariness. A chair scraped harshly. Then there was a complete well-like silence. "I said get out from behind that bar."

From the moment he had walked toward the saloon, he knew it was a calculated risk. He could go in shooting or play it this way. It was that or ride out of town and pretend he had never heard of Three Wells.

"Who—" The single word was all the astonished man got out.

Sul's hands shot across the bar, fastened on the shirt and soft flesh under the armpits. With one heave, he pulled the yelping man from his feet and sent him sliding head first over the bar and to the floor. The movement turned him so that he faced the room. The eyes of every one in the room were on the four at the card table. Carefully, the dealer put aside the undealt cards. His finger tips rested lightly on the table's edge.

"Which one of you is Morse?" Sul waited.

"I'm Morse. What's it to you?" The bearded man rested the heels of his hands on his hips near the two guns slung there.

"You're under arrest." Sul spoke carefully, slowly.

Someone laughed, but it was a nervous, uncertain sound. Morse stared incredulously at Sul. The bartender picked himself up and edged away.

"You've got to be a Ranger." Morse spoke almost regretfully. "No one but a Ranger would make a fool play like this." His face broke into a wolfish smile. "I ain't never had me a Ranger before."

"On your feet." Sul ignored the remark. "On your feet and drop your belts."

"You figure on doin' this alone, Ranger?" Morse shook his head bemusedly.

The tinkle of breaking glass came as a sharp explosion. The head of every man in the room, with the exception of Sul's swiveled automatically. A rifle was thrust through the jagged hole and above it Pop's face was mildly reproving. During the second when attention was not on him, Sul pulled his gun. Morse turned and looked into it and his mouth sagged foolishly.

"Out of those chairs, the four of you, one at a time." Sul felt a rising tension. He wasn't really running a bluff, but this was a real fair imitation of one. Morse and the others had no way of knowing how many Rangers were outside.

Morse's tongue flicked out over his lips. "We only bin horsin' around some, Ranger. Maybe we got a little rough." The man waited a moment, patently hoping that the explanation would satisfy. Then, his left hand moved slowly to the buckle of the belt.

The guns hit the floor, one by one, with heavy thuds. Sul expelled his breath slowly. His gun flicked toward the door and Morse, followed by three dazed, unbelieving companions, shuffled toward it.

"This place is closed." Sul spoke to the room at large. "Those of you who live in Three Wells go home. The rest of you get out of town fast."

"Yeah, sure, Ranger." An unidentified voice agreed. "We didn't have nothin' to do with this, anyhow. Just hung around to see the fun."

Sul ignored the explanation. He fell in behind Morse and his trio, marching them in a dejected parade to the jail. Pop joined Sul as the group moved down the street. From the stores and buildings the townspeople ducked out, timid but curious rabbits to watch and gape in disbelief and wonder.

Sul prodded Morse and his companions into the cell and turned a heavy key in the lock.

"What are you goin' to do now, Ranger?" Morse actually seemed to find a measure of comfort in the barred door that separated him from the Ranger.

"Leave you here." The statement was cheerful. "After the people of the town get their nerve back they'll probably hang you. If they don't, I'll come back and do it myself. What did you think you were doing, Morse?"

The man seemed honestly puzzled. He looked at his friends as though he had never seen them before and was mildly surprised to be in their company. He pushed back his hat and scratched at his head.

"Go on, tell me about it." Sul's voice was cold.

"It just sort of grew, Ranger." Morse fumbled for an explanation. "After the sheriff, no one made much of a move to stop us. The whole town seemed so scared that we just said, why not? That's how it happened. No one stood up to us. They made it easy." He seemed upset over the citizens' spinelessness, blaming them for the trouble. "It was almost comical, how they folded up."

"Well, have a good laugh." Sul turned away and hung the cell's key on a nail.

Later, in the lobby of the only hotel, Sul faced a gathering of the town's men who shifted unhappily beneath his accusing eyes.

"A whole town lets four bullies come in and take over without lifting a hand. What's the matter with you folks?"

"We're not used to trouble, Captain." Keeler, the grocer, still wearing his apron, explained for the others who nodded apologetically. "Three Wells is a peaceful sort of a town. After they killed Walt, there just didn't seem to be anyone who wanted to stand up to them. That includes me." He made the admission unhappily. "We figured they'd get their fill an' move on."

"Trouble doesn't generally move on unless someone gives it a nudge." Sul had the feeling that they were waiting for him to tell them what to do next. "You'd better get together and appoint a new sheriff. There are four men in jail. I can't take them with me where I'm going and there's nobody to send with them to Austin."

"We'll handle it, Captain." Someone spoke from the back of the room. "We'll handle it fast and the way it oughta be done. I guess most of us feel pretty foolish about what happened."

Sul nodded. There was no point in pressing it. The men were ready to stand on their own feet now.

"I guess we at least ought to say thanks for what you done—what we should have done ourselves." A man stepped forward and offered his hand. He grinned a little shamefacedly. "I don't know how I'm ever goin' to live this down with my wife."

They all filed past then, eager to shake hands, mumble their thanks and be gone. The nightmare had no reality now and each man told himself that given a little more time he would have stood up to Morse and his gang.

Sul and Pop waited until the lobby was cleared. The owner was behind his desk, briskly eager to be about his normal business.

"Anything you want, Captain. The best rooms, on the house." He rubbed his hands together happily.

Later, in the large double room, Sul lifted a dripping face from the china wash basin and turned to Pop.

"I almost forgot." He rubbed soap from his ears with a towel. "This thing cost me two dollars for the drink I paid for at the bar. A real expensive day."

Chapter Sixteen

Park Manning snaked the long whip out over the backs of the two teams and the wagon jolted forward. He was second in line. Behind him, each waiting its turn to move, three more of the covered vehicles were spaced out from a barge moored to the shore. Beneath the tarpaulins were cases of Austrian rifles, a forty-eight-and-one-half-inch weapon of .54 caliber, complete with bayonet and sling.

All night, men had been at work loading from the

barges. Now, in the first smoky streakings of dawn the convoy was headed southwest in the general direction of Monterrey. Park leaned from the seat and looked back. The soldier-guard on the wagon with him stared straight ahead. Directly behind Park, Dewey worked his jaws over a quid of tobacco, one foot cocked against the heavy brake rod. He spat and lifted a hand in salute.

In addition to the armed guard on each wagon, a mounted squad of Mexican cavalry flanked the train. They were crack troops, smartly-uniformed and well-disciplined, a sharp contrast to the sooty-appearing soldiers usually seen on the streets or in the cantinas of Matamoros. Park wondered where they had come from, but a question to the guard at his side resulted in nothing more than a shrug.

Manning lit a twisted, oily cheroot while thinking over the puzzle. The directions he had been given wouldn't take them upstream along the Rio Grande as he had supposed they would. They were heading inland on this southwesterly course and that sure wasn't going to put the rifles into the hands of Indians in Texas.

There had been no time or opportunity to get word to the rendezvous at Willow Bend. He and Dewey had been awakened in the middle of the night by a soldier who had banged his rifle butt against the door of their room at the *posada*. Their employment had not been an offer but an order. No mistaking that. At the river bank, they had seen the first of the barges warped ashore. The young chief of Matamoros police was standing to one side watching the operation.

Pretending a sense of injury, Park had walked up to confront him. "Are we being arrested again?"

The man shook his head. "This is the employment about which I spoke." His eyebrows lifted with an expression of amused irony. "I must apologize for the hour of your awakening."

"What are the wages? Where are we going?" Manning studied the barges.

"The wages will be fully commensurate with your labor." Again there was a disturbing sarcasm in the glance and intonation. "The destination is unimportant. You will take your orders from the lieutenant of the patrol. All that is required is that you drive and maintain your place in the train." He turned away abruptly and strode to where a man with a tally sheet was checking off the rifle cases as they were brought ashore.

Park glanced at Dewey and grinned. "Whatever we get is gravy since we're already drawing a dollar a day from the Rangers."

"You know something?" Dewey was unhappy. "We could get our heads blowed off on this job an' us bein' more or less, like they say, innocent bystanders."

This had already occurred to Manning. Assuming that they found no way to get word to Sul that they were with the train they were stuck on the drivers' seats of these wagons. The fording, when it was made, might well be in the face of Ranger or even Army opposition. No one was going to stop and ask questions when the shooting started. All wagons and drivers would look the same. There wasn't much they could do but ride it out and take their chances. He whistled dolefully. There were a hell of a lot of guns back there and trouble for Texas in every one of them.

As he watched the last of the wagons disappear across the slight incline, the *Jefe de Policia* laughed quietly to himself. The two Texas Rangers were where they could make no trouble. He had known their identity from almost the first day of their arrival in Matamoros. It had amused him to assume a stupidity and ignorance. Divisions in the border town were few. He could have kept them in jail but there would have been no jest in that. To have them drive wagons to their own execution. That stimulated his appreciation for the ridiculous. The lieutenant of cavalry carried with him a letter to Corbel revealing the presence of the two Rangers. The general would dispose of them. In the meantime, they were where they could cause no trouble, make no reports. Also, and this pleased him mightily as the final touch, he had secured a couple of drivers for nothing.

Chapter Seventeen

At Willow Bend, Sul scratched a rough map in the dirt with a twig. The Rangers were hunkered down about him in a tight circle.

"The best thing we can do at the moment is to try and guess what Corbel will do." He made a series of small X marks. "He could get the wagons across here, here, there and there. I don't figure he would go much farther north. The banks are too steep. Even so, there's a lot of territory to cover and we're going to have to do it alone."

"Did you ever think that maybe Iron Shirt and his braves might cross the river and pick up the guns themselves?" a Ranger interrupted. "That way they could come back armed and shootin'."

Sul shook his head. "That would be too big a movement of Indians; five or six hundred, maybe. I don't think Corbel would take a chance on having that many Indians loose in Mexico. They just might raid a few Mexican towns for the hell of it before they came back to run loose in Texas. No, I think Corbel will make a rendezvous on this side." He paused, trying to put himself in Corbel's place. Also, he was worried at not hearing from Indian Charley. The half-breed had simply disappeared. He was with the Indians, but where? On the way back from Fort Clark he and Pop hadn't picked up one Indian sign. The tribes had vanished. Cattle raiding had stopped. They were holed up somewhere. But where?

The men had received with indifference the news that they were to get no help from the Army. They were accustomed to going it alone. A few even resented the idea of Army intrusion in what was strictly a matter for Texas and Texans.

Sul tossed the twig away and stood up. His glance

swept the circle. "Yancey," he was brusque without meaning to be, impersonal because that was his way. "I want you to ride into Brownsville and take a message to John Drago."

Yancey flushed at the order. There, again, was the implication that he was fitted for nothing more than the most routine of tasks; the trivial duties that carried with them no danger.

Sul appeared not to notice the sullen mask on his brother's face. "We're going to need help. Maybe Drago can recruit some men."

The group broke up, the Rangers drifting away, leaving the two brothers alone. Yancey stared stonily at Sul.

"Drago is a big rancher outside of Brownsville. He's in town at lot. If you can't find him there, someone will give you directions to his place. He has a lot of influence and he'll understand what it will mean if Iron Shirt's warriors get on a rampage in Texas. Tell him I want all the men he can get together to ride with us until this thing is over. We need supplies, too. I've got a list you can take to Chance Porter's store. I'll sign for it all or get John Drago to do it." Yancey's anger mounted as Sul ticked the instructions off.

"I didn't join the Rangers to do a messenger boy's job."

Sul looked up in quick astonishment. The tone and the objection were petulant. "You'll carry out your orders the same as everyone else. What's the matter with you, anyhow?"

"I'll tell you what's the matter. I'm getting pretty sick of this, Sul. Go here. Wait there. Do this. Do that. It's kid stuff. When I had a chance to get into things and maybe see some action with Manning you kept me here." He regarded Sul defiantly, legs spread aggressively, hands loose at his side.

"I'm sorry your feelings are hurt. I just try to pick the best men for the job."

"And I'm the best man to run errands and go to the grocery store?"

"I didn't say that and I'm not going to argue with you."

"Then you'll have to fight me, man to man."

Sul shook his head unhappily. "Don't you think it's about time you began to act like a man, then?"

Without further words, Yancey made a headlong rush. His head was down, arms swinging. That was the way he and Sul used to fight as youngsters back in Virginia. They'd flail at each other with the elder doing nothing more than trying to protect himself. As Yancey came into him, Sul stepped to one side and clipped him on the head near the ear. It wasn't a savage blow. As Yancey staggered, Sul's hand fastened on his shoulder, jerking him to a halt.

"Now you listen to me!" There was undisguised anger and impatience in the command. "Everything we do from this minute on is important. It can't all be circus stuff with guns blazing and Rangers riding hell for leather. I'm not going to dress up every order I give you to satisfy some ridiculous vanity. Getting word to Drago is as necessary as anything we do right now. I want you to take it."

Yancey was breathing heavily. "Sure. I know. So I'll be out of the way and safe if anything happens here."

"You'll take my orders, Yancey, or turn in your badge."

"You'd like that. It's what you've been aiming for all along. You never wanted me here."

"That's right." Sul was undisturbed. "I didn't want you here, but not for the reason you think. But," he continued, "you are here and you'll do what I ask."

"You don't ask, Sul. You tell people." Already, Yancey was ashamed of his outburst, but he didn't know how to retreat from his position with grace. So he continued to be stubborn. All of his life he had tried to measure up to Sul and only succeeded in making himself look and feel foolish. "You're the mailed fist without the glove. You're ramrod stiff because you don't know any other way."

Sul could almost hear the childish treble of a day long past and he smiled one of his rare smiles. When he spoke his voice was softer.

"When you see Drago tell him what we know. He'll understand what has to be done. I've already sent word to Austin from Fort Clark. They'll send us as many Rangers as they can spare, and that may be none." He paused and laughed softly. The stubbornness was leaving Yancey's face. "You'll get all the fireworks and excitement you want before this is over. There should be enough fighting to last you a lifetime and," he added soberly, "I hope it is a long one."

"All right, Sul." The agreement was a half-hearted one. Always in an encounter with Sul he felt deflated. "I'll find Drago and take your message." He hesitated as though to add something and then turned away, walking to the line where the horses were picketed.

Sul watched him for a moment; his expression was half-wistful, half-regretful. Then he went back to stand beside the small fire and pour himself a cup of the strong, black coffee.

As Yancey followed the river which would lead him into Brownsville, his resentment evaporated. He was a Ranger and on a Ranger's job that needed doing. If he hadn't been there, Sul would have sent someone else. So, he guessed, it wasn't a personal thing after all.

In the softness of the day with its dappled sunshine and pleasant bird sounds, he experienced a sense of unreality. Back home, Indian fighting was a phrase that, somehow, evoked a scene of gaudy pageantry, of swirling combat with feathered and bedecked savages howling their fury from nimble ponies, of plumed lances, singing bows and whining arrows. No one suggested that it was this way— sweat, long stretches of monotony, a scrubby camp at Willow Bend. He laughed softly to himself, thinking of the envy of his friends when he had ridden away from Virginia to join these legendary Rangers in Texas. Someone ought to tell them how it really was. Bad and sometimes raw food in your belly, a stinking blanket to sleep in, weeks at a time without a change of clothing and a rare bath in a muddy stream. Always you were outnumbered by the miles to be patrolled, and the people were never satisfied that you were doing enough.

He reined up a few miles outside of Brownsville. Scraggly palmettos dotted the landscape, growing by the river which found its way into the Gulf of Mexico. It was a flat, warm land and deceptively peaceful. It looked like fine cotton country. A covey of quail took off from beneath a cover and he followed the pattern with appreciative eyes. It didn't seem possible that Brownsville could be the hell-roaring town described to him by Pop Warner. Once, the old man had said, fourteen rustlers had been hung in one day in the market place. Juan Cortina had raided it from Mexico and the Texans had replied by going into Mata-moros and shooting the place up. The riffraff of a dozen states congregated here and brewed their deviltry.

In town, he went directly to the Brown House, as Sul directed, and made inquiries about John Drago.

"He's in town," the clerk told him. "Came yesterday." He glanced at the key rack. "I ain't seen him this morn-ing, yet. Likely enough he's out on some business. You can wait or go out looking. Drago ain't a hard man to find."

Yancey nodded. "I'd like a room and a chance at a bath. When Mr. Drago comes in will you tell him for me that I've got a message for him from Sul Carter. Could I get something to eat after I wash up?"

The clerk looked at a wall clock. "Dinner's in half an hour. You can get a bath if you want it. That'll be fifty cents extra, sixty cents if you ain't got your own soap." He handed Yancey a key. "Right up them steps an' turn to your right."

Yancey nodded and moved from the desk. As he did, his eyes swept the flight of stairs leading to the second floor and his mouth half-opened with astonishment.

Followed by a maid, Anna De Lacey paused on the narrow landing and for a moment their eyes met and held. Her hesitation was brief, almost imperceptible. Then, she continued on down the steps with a detached serenity, as though her feet were not touching the boards.

"Yancey." She extended her hand graciously. "This is a surprise." Her smile was fleeting and, he thought, just a little uncertain. "What brings you to Brownsville?"

As he touched her finger tips, Yancey checked himself from asking the same question. Hers had been a mere pleasantry. His would be rudeness.

"You have suffered no unpleasant effects from your misadventure at San Sebastian?" She looked up brightly.

"No, Ma'm." As always, she made him feel awkward and tongue-tied.

"That is good. Frequently there is a *malaise* afterwards."

The hotel door opened and a liveried groom stood in the opening. At the sight of Anna De Lacey he removed his hat quickly and spoke to her respectfully in Spanish, then stepped aside, holding the door ajar for her passage.

"I am visiting friends in Mexico." Her hand rested on his arm. "Will you walk with me to my carriage?"

Outside, lending an almost flamboyant note to the dusty street and weatherbeaten buildings, the heavy coach of Andre Corbel waited. There was no mistaking it nor the significance now of the word "friends." Yancey experienced a sudden unreasonable torment.

"You must not look shocked." She spoke so softly that her words were all but inaudible. Her eyes were solemn but a faint, wistful smile touched her lips for a second. "Nor wear your feelings like a badge upon your sleeve."

"I'm not shocked," he defended himself stoutly. "I guess I'm not even surprised."

"It is a way of life, I suspect, with which you are unfamiliar. Unfortunately, some things must be accepted for what they are." They crossed the boardwalk. "But," and he could have sworn she was laughing at him, "it is not a situation without precedent, I assure you."

He handed her into the coach. Any other woman, girl, would have been embarrassed, would have made elaborate explanations which would have fooled no one. She treated the situation as a simple matter of fact. The maid entered and took the opposite seat, facing backwards, and the groom closed the door. Her face was framed by the open window.

"Please give my regards to your brother."

"I'll do that, Ma'am." The harshness of his voice surprised him. "Give my regards to the general."

"That was unnecessary," she rebuked him quietly. "Un-

necessary and a little *gauche*. I believe Virginians make a
tradition of their gallantry and courtesy."

"I'm sorry. I guess I just didn't think. Or maybe I did,
and that makes it worse."

"I forgive you. I am even a little touched and flattered,
Mr. Carter." Her smile was radiant. Then, she nodded to
the maid who rapped sharply on the ceiling of the com-
partment.

The coach jerked and then rolled swiftly away followed
by small whirls of dust from the wheels and hooves.
Yancey stood looking after it. He knew he had conducted
himself badly but instead of remorse he felt only an
unreasonable anger. He was annoyed with himself. So, she
was Corbel's mistress. This much she had intimated the
first night they met at Don Porfirio's. "My protector," she
had called Corbel. It should have been enough to let him
know how things stood. He had to be hit over the head
with it not only at San Sebastian but, again, here in
Brownsville. Anyhow, who was he to question what she
did?

While he bathed and shaved, he tried to dismiss the
image of Anna De Lacey from his mind. He guessed that
the arrangement between her and Corbel was common
enough among foreigners, who were notoriously loose.
Why was he behaving as though she was being violated?
Sul had suggested that the range of San Sebastian was
being used as a gathering depot for the cattle that eventually found their way into Mexico. There wasn't any real
proof, but a thousand head could be concealed within its
broad reaches. If this was true, she was in the thing up to
her neck. She and Corbel were a pair in the dirty business.

When Yancey went back downstairs the clerk pointed
to a man at a table in the dining room. Yancey crossed to
him and John Drago's face lighted with pleasure at the
mention of Sul Carter's name. He motioned Yancey to a
chair and continued to eat while he listened to Sul's message.

When Yancey had finished, Drago pushed his plate
aside and lit a cigar. "We've got sort of a town militia

here, but aside from parading and getting drunk on the Fourth of July, I wouldn't want to count on them for much more. I'll get word out to some of the other ranchers. They've got the most to lose with Indian trouble so we can count on them to do the most. You tell Sul I'll do the best I can and come down myself with as many men as I can round up."

Drago's acceptance of the situation was so casual that Yancey wondered if the man really understood what was about to happen. "I've got a supply list here." He took a paper from his pocket and spread it out for Drago. "Sul said you'd sign for the stuff."

"We'll walk over to Chance Porter's." Drago wiped a smear of ham gravy from his chin. "You eat first. I've got some things to do and I'll come back by the time you're ready."

Yancey put away an enormous meal of fried fish, steak, eggs, ham and grits and hot biscuits. As he ate, his mind ranged over many things. Anna De Lacey. Park and Manning somewhere in Mexico, maybe right across the river. A real Indian war that still, to him, had the quality of unreality. He was smoking a cigar over his second cup of coffee when John Drago returned. He dropped into a chair.

"If you're ready we'll go see Chance. He can put the stuff together and we'll roll it down in a wagon to Willow Bend tomorrow. How many men has Sul got with him?"

"Fifteen."

Drago chuckled. "Fifteen men and Sul Carter's ready to take on old Iron Shirt. What do you suppose has got into these jaspers? I mean the Indians. They can't win. In the end, they've got to admit they're licked, but a lot of good men have got to die first proving it to them. Sometimes I wonder if this country'll ever get civilized. You favor your brother some." He made the last statement irrelevantly. "A real good man, Sul Carter."

When they were finished at the general store, Yancey thanked Drago for his help and said good-bye. Everything Sul wanted would be loaded and sent. There wasn't anything left for him to do but go back to Willow Bend. He wondered if Sul expected him back the same day. Then, his jaw set stubbornly. He hadn't said so. A man could use his own judgment, then. "I think I'll just look over the town and maybe kick up my heels some tonight." He chuckled to himself. To fortify this decision he strode into a saloon and drank a whiskey, gagging a little at the raw taste of the stuff.

Sightseeing in Brownsville was limited. He walked along the river and along the Gulf shore and the day plodded on. To accelerate things, he made two or three more saloon stops and discovered that the town took on a brighter aspect. With the approach of evening, it became almost gay. Music seemed louder than he had ever heard it. The saloon girls were beautiful and amiable companions. When his spirits flagged slightly, he buoyed them with another straight whiskey. He stood shoulder to shoulder with the men lining the bars and danced a *paso doble* with a jet-eyed Mexican girl who, although she spoke no English, seemed to have not the slightest trouble in understanding him. In fact, she appeared completely enchanted by his charm and wit.

Yancey left an erratic trail that led from the larger saloons to the cantinas down by the river. He leaned against a nicked and stained counter now and surveyed himself with owlish surprise. The reflection in the mirror seemed slightly cockeyed. He ordered tequila and drank it in the Mexican fashion with salt and lime until his mouth felt puckered. He listened with a foggy appreciation to the *mariachis* as they sang a lament of *"El Caminante,"* meaning the stroller, the walker, or, he guessed, the wanderer. It filled him with sadness.

"Let me buy you a drink, Ranger."

Yancey had a little difficulty locating the man although he was at his side. "How'd you know I was a Ranger?"

"That tin star you're wearin' ain't exactly a disguise."

Yancey peered down at the badge pinned to his shirt and then with clumsy fingers unpinned it. He had a vague idea he shouldn't be wearing it so openly on this excursion. A drunken Ranger didn't inspire confidence. Of course, he wasn't drunk yet but it just might slip up on him.

"I guess even a Ranger's got to get it out of his system now and then." The stranger crowded in closer to the bar.

There was, Yancey thought, a rare understanding in his chance acquaintance. "My name's Carter. Yancey Carter." He was going to offer his hand but the floor tipped and he gripped the bar's edge instead. "I'm havin' a little tear for myself."

His companion nodded sympathetically. "If I was on a toot," he suggested, "I'd pick a better place than this." His hand swept to indicate the dingy room. "Take across the river, now. I know some places where a young buck could really have some fun. You any relation to Captain Sullivan Carter?"

Yancey considered this question. Everyone, apparently, knew Sul. Word of this could get back to him. So what did he care? "I'm his brother. I'm his *kid* brother, he'd tell you." He made room for another man who edged in alongside of him.

"Let me buy you a drink then. Sul and I are old friends. Yes sir, sure enough old friends."

They measured the colorless tequila into their glasses. "Is it true that they make this stuff out of cactus?" Yancey peered into his glass.

"Boy!" A heavy hand clapped his back jovially. "Can't you taste the spikes in it? Toss it down." The man smacked his lips. "It sure enough was comical what happened to Sul, I hear."

"Like what?" Yancey's eyes refused to focus.

"Like those busters who strung him up an' left his horse to hang him."

Yancey laughed suddenly at the recollection of Sul, trussed and helpless. "They should have known better, mister," he snickered. "It didn't work. No one can hang a state, and that's what Sul is. The whole damn state of Texas." He started to laugh again and then halted. His head turned slowly and he stared at the man. "How did you know about Sul—about the hanging?"

"Oh! I guess I just heard it around." There was a

sudden wariness about the stranger now. "Have another drink, Ranger."

A faint prickle of warning ran along Yancey's back. The alcoholic fog lifted slightly. There was something funny here but he wasn't sure what.

"Drink up an' we'll go across the river an' maybe find us a real fandango."

Yancey shook his head and pushed away the proffered bottle. "You know something, mister." He spoke slowly and with difficulty. "I think you're a liar. Nobody knew about that except Sul and me and," he progressed slowly from fact to fact, "and the man who did it." He moved with annoyance as the man on his left pressed against him until he was wedged tightly between them. "You're crowding me, friend." He spoke sharply over his shoulder and then turned again to his new acquaintance. "I still think you're a liar, mister. No one could know about it. I think your name's got to be Rale Latham."

Something from the back exploded against his head. He felt a sudden weakness in his legs and his knees buckled. He sagged, straining frantically to hold himself upright. He carried one, clear picture with him into the swirling blackness—Rale Latham's grinning face.

He awoke without any recollection of what had happened to him or the passage of time. He was lying face down on the rattling bed of a wagon, his face pressed into a pile of foul and moldy sacks. When he attempted to move his arms he discovered they were bound at the wrists. With difficulty, he rolled over on his back and stared into a star-shot sky. His head ached intolerably and the fumes of liquor clouded his mind. Dimly, he could see the heads and shoulders of a couple of riders who paced their animals to the progress of the wagon which jolted and heaved sickeningly, churning his stomach. Slowly, he tried to force himself into a sitting position, but without the use of his hands he couldn't make it and he fell back weakly. A sudden voice brought back what had happened with unhappy clarity.

"We got us a real chicken of a Ranger to pluck." The accompanying laughter was harsh and without humor.

Yancey remembered now. The cantina and Latham. "Only," the unseen speaker continued, "the old man wants him for a while. So take good care of him."

"Who," Yancey wondered miserably, "was the old man?" It was easy enough to understand Latham. He was getting even with Sul. But, and this bothered him, if he only wanted to get hunk with Sul, why hadn't they just dragged him out of the cantina and finished him off somewhere along the empty stretches of the river front? It was this trip that puzzled him. Where was he bound? His mouth tasted like a skunk had nested there. He wished he had a drink of water. He wished he was back at Willow Bend or, better still, in Virginia. No matter how he got out of this, he would never live it down. A fine Ranger he was, a credit to the troop. The wagon hit a rut, his head banged through the sacking to the timber and he thought he had split his skull. After awhile, misery and the hangover drove him into a fitful sleep of exhaustion.

Sul and John Drago stood talking beside the wagon which had come out with supplies and ammunition from Brownsville.

"And," Sul was gravely thoughtful, "you didn't see him after that?"

Drago shook his head. "No, I figured he'd be on his way back here after he looked around town for a while. There isn't a lot to do there, as you know, except to get drunk. Maybe that's what he did."

"It doesn't seem likely." Sul dismissed the suggestion. He was worried. This wasn't like Yancey. He was bullheaded and self-conscious about being a younger brother and under Sul's command but he wouldn't absent himself deliberately. He was enough of a Ranger to come back and make his report.

"I'll ask around when I get back." Drago wasn't particularly concerned. "He's probably sleeping one off at the hotel. I've got fifteen men for you, Sul. They'll be coming in during the day and I'll be back tomorrow. You got any definite plan?"

"I wish I did have." Sul stared at the buzzards wheeling

high overhead, planing easily through a cloudless sky. "When I hear from Manning and Dewey I'll know more. If Indian Charley lets me know where the tribes are I'll have something to go on. Meanwhile, since I can't read the music I'll have to play it by ear."

Chapter Eighteen

Within the concealing mountains, the headmen of the tribes had sat about a council fire throughout the night. As they peered thoughtfully into the flames, each held a silent communion with his own particular spirit. Now, although few words had been spoken, decisions had been made. Iron Shirt gave the signal for the general talk to begin.

"We have waited long enough," the Apache, Running Wolf, stated. "We will take no more cattle until he, with the double tongue, delivers the guns as promised. My braves are restless, and although they do not speak, I can read the question in their eyes. They ask: Is it for nothing that we have made this white man wealthy in many cattle?"

There was a general murmur of agreement. Iron Shirt waited until it died down. "I do not have much faith in this white man but I believe he will keep his promise about the guns. He will do this because he needs our warriors to help him in his plan. He will do it because he knows that if he does not, he will no longer be safe anywhere. He has said he would send word when the wagons are ready to cross. We will wait a little longer."

"What of the white men who wear the stars of silver? Those who camp now beside the river?" Yellow Arrow voiced a question in the minds of many.

Iron Shirt nodded. The movements, the number and the patrol of the Rangers was known to them all. "They must be destroyed," he said, "before the wagons start to cross. They are few in numbers but great fighters and brave men. We will make our plans to fall upon them by surprise but not until we have word of the wagons. To do it in advance would only bring more of their number and, perhaps, the soldiers, also. For a while, we leave them alone, as though we do not know they are there."

A shrill, high burbling sound split the morning, carrying with it terror and maddening, unendurable pain. A death cry, it quavered and echoed, then stopped abruptly.

The men listened silently, as though they had not heard. Savages though they were, they were somewhat awed at times by the ferocity of the women with a captive. They made an orgiastic rite of torture, inciting themselves to paroxysms of sadistic fury unmatched by the cruelest of men. They became drunk on another's pain.

What remained of Indian Charley lay upon the ground while the shrieking women poked at his mutilated body with lances and cut his skin into ribbons with sharp stones. What was left barely resembled a man, now. Pointed sticks, taken from the fire when they glowed redly, had been thrust into his ears. Blood continued to drip from the empty cavity of his mouth. The tongue had been ripped out. Flies were already gathering on the vacant sockets that had once held eyes. He was past all agony now but the women could not resist further mutilation. They howled their excitement, slashing at the lifeless body, working themselves into a frenzied ecstasy. They tore their own hair and ripped at their clothing until they danced naked above the waist, screaming and slobbering.

The men in the circle listened for further sound. It was good. The slinking dog who had come among them as one of their own was dead. He would spy no more for the whites. It had been an opinion among some of those at the council that the body be sent back to the whites gathered at the river as a challenge. Iron Shirt had argued against this. It would be an empty gesture now. Let them think their spy was still among the tribes. Keep the Rangers waiting for his report. They would be puzzled and uncertain when he failed to return. It was better that the

Rangers did not suspect that the tribes knew of their presence along the river. Iron Shirt picked up a handful of dirt and tossed it upon the dwindling flames of the fire as a signal that the council talk was over.

Anna De Lacey and Andre Corbel sat across from each other at a small table. Before them was an inlaid board and a set of exquisitely wrought silver chessmen. As Corbel studied his play, the angry sound of argument filtered into the room from the courtyard. There were the thuds of blows and excited shouts.

Anna shrugged delicately and made a small gesture of annoyance. "Must those mongrels of yours be so noisy, Andre?"

Corbel chuckled softly. "I surround myself with lean and hungry men. It is a good sign that they snarl and prowl among each other. I want them kept angry and in a fighting humor."

"I am weary of chess." Anna stood up suddenly and walked to one of the narrow, barred windows. She stood looking out upon the dusty court with its rough and bearded men. One lay upon the ground, battered into insensibility. "Sometimes," she seemed to speak to herself, "I feel myself a prisoner here. I think you dream upon a too grandiose scale. We are made captive by it."

"It is a good dream." He reached for a wine decanter on a low table. "It is a dream of empire which, throughout history, has been shared by many men." He sipped his wine and leaned back to study with pleasure her clear profile. "You wear a tiara of beauty, my dear Anna. In time it may become a crown."

She laughed then, vibrantly, richly. "If I do not lose my head first; an experience which, throughout history, has also been shared by many women. I will say this for you, Andre, your scheming is exciting. It keeps me from being bored. However, I think you may underestimate the Americans. They will not give up so easily."

"Come here." He stretched out his hand and after a moment she crossed to his side. With a heavy playfulness he drew her to his lap. "You are a woman for which intrigue was made. I think you delight in it as much as I."

She submitted to his caress absently, a faraway look in her eyes. Sensing her detachment he shook her shoulders roughly.

"It does not please me to have you thinking of someone else while in my arms."

"A boy," she confessed, "and since he is only a boy you need not be concerned. It is too late and I have grown too old in wisdom."

"It will be better if you do not return to Texas." His fingers moved about the delicate nape of her neck. "San Sebastian has served its purpose. We will need it no longer. There is nothing left for the Indians to steal."

"I think Captain Carter suspected the use to which I had put San Sebastian. Fortunately, the day he was there the herd had already been driven to Mexico. There was nothing for him to see." She leaned slightly away in order to look into his face. "I remain here." It was not a question.

"Where else would you go, my dear Anna?" There was an unmistakable coarseness in the query.

"Of course." She did not seem to be offended. "Where would I go? A stray cat does not voluntarily leave a warm fireside." She sighed. "I think it is your delicacy that charms me, Andre. What of my people at San Sebastian? They are not happy or welcome in Texas."

"Leave them there." The order was abrupt.

"Of course. I had forgotten." She stood up and smoothed out her skirt. "They have served their purpose."

"You seem to enjoy measuring my temper today, Anna." He glowered at her.

"Can it be measured, Andre?" She laughed then. "We are bickering, are we not? Such a domestic pastime. That is the price we must pay for too much confinement." She reseated herself, but this time on the arm of another chair. "You have been restless these past two days. For what do you wait?"

"The shipment of arms from Matamoros. These must be delivered to the Indians across the river. Then I sit back and wait for the massacre to begin. When it is over,

General Andre Corbel will ride across the river to restore order and impose the law. I will have my own army. The Indians will be running short of ammunition and will not be resupplied. They will submit and Texas will be mine."

"You really believe that, Andre?" She regarded him wonderingly.

"Of course I believe it," he shouted. "I am no man of petty dreams. I must believe it. Do you understand?"

Chapter Nineteen

The village was no more than a double row of cramped adobe huts on both sides of the road. The inhabitants stood silently in their doorways, watching the arrival of the wagon train with blank curiosity. The wagons filled the street. Boys carried huge earthenware ollas of water to fill a trough for the horses. The drivers loafed upon their seats smoking and flicking their whips at the children who crowded about begging for tobacco.

At the head of the column, Rale Latham stood with the lieutenant of cavalry. With them, his wrists no longer bound, Yancey waited in an attitude of cowed defiance. After listening to Latham, the officer turned.

"How will you make it with us, *joven*; tied as a captive or riding quietly and obediently? It is a matter of indifference to me."

"You don't have to tie me up. I won't run away. I don't know where I am, anyhow."

"Bueno." The officer shrugged. "We will put you in one of the wagons. If you try to escape I will have you shot. It is simple, *verdad?*"

"You're right it's simple," Yancey thought bitterly. "And I'm sure enough simple-minded to be caught this way." He kicked the toe of his boot irritably at the hard ground and then followed the officer toward the lead wagon. He wondered if this meeting with the train was accidental or prearranged. Suddenly, on the seat of the second wagon, he caught sight of Park Manning. An involuntary cry of recognition sprang to his lips but was nailed there by Park's gaze of steely malevolence. Yancey had been on the point of ruining everything. "I don't guess I'll ever learn," he thought unhappily. This was something, though. He felt a quick surge of pride and admiration. This was better than Sul had hoped for, a couple of Rangers with the train.

The lieutenant spoke in rapid Spanish to the driver and soldier-guard on the seat. Grumbling a little, the soldier moved off and into the wagon. The officer motioned Yancey to the empty place. As he sat down, he felt a vicious jab of the guard's rifle in his back. The warning was plain enough.

When the watering was finished the train moved on through the village. It was late afternoon when they halted. The wagons moved into a tight circle and guards were posted about it. The horses were taken care of and then the occupants of each wagon set about the business of preparing their meal individually. It was simple and primitive. Tortillas were scorched over the flames, a small pot of beans and meat set to warm at the fireside. Yancey waited hungrily and listened. Several times he heard the words estancia, Corbel, Corbel's ranch. That, then, was where he was being sent and Corbel was "the old man" Latham had spoken of. Even so, this didn't make much sense. Why would Corbel want him? He glanced across the circle to where Park and Dewey were stretched out lazily by their fire. They ignored him.

With a casualness they did not feel, Park and Dewey settled down beyond the drivers and guards. As they rolled beans and meat into tortillas they talked quietly.

"I wouldn't have been more surprised if Sul himself had come ridin' up." Dewey mixed the words with the food in his mouth. "What you suppose happened?"

"It's a cinch Sul wouldn't have sent Yancey in alone." Park spat out a piece of gristle. "So we got to figure Yancey had himself took."

"But why? That's what I'd like to know? Who'd want to grab Yancey?"

Park shook his head. The situation puzzled him, also. He didn't like it. With luck, though, Yancey's presence could turn out to be a help. "If we could get him loose," Manning mused, "not right now but later, when the wagons are on the last move for the river, then we could get word to Sul about the direction. That way we could stay with the train right up to the end. We could even start shootin' from the inside when Sul an' the others whack down. It'd surprise 'em some."

"How we goin' to talk with him?" Dewey let his gaze stray to where Yancey sat.

"We're not going to try, now. Not even if we get a chance. Stay away from him. It's a cinch the lieutenant knows who he is. So, we don't. Understand? We never saw him before."

"Sure. I wasn't goin' to try." Dewey grunted and lazily rolled over on his back. "You do the schemin'. I just wish we'd had time to buy us a jug of that tequila before we left Matamoros. It'd sure go good now. Eatin' makes me thirsty."

Sul concealed his disappointment as his glance moved over the four men who had drawn themselves up before him. Out of a possible fifteen that Drago had promised, only these had shown up. They were big, clumsy men who clutched their rifles with tight unfamiliarity. They were small ranchers, farmers really, who had probably never used their guns on anything more dangerous than a coyote. They were apprehensive and not the fighting men he needed so desperately. They could have no idea what they were in for. He wanted to say: Go home. This isn't a job for you. But, he knew they wouldn't understand and it would shame them.

"I guess John Drago told you everything I know and that's damned little at the moment." He forced a smile, aware of their uncertainty. "Thank you for coming. We'll do our best."

One of them shuffled awkwardly, swallowed hard and

forced himself to speak. "I guess what you really expected, Cap'n, was border fighters, some fast an' handy guns.
I don't suppose any of us here has ever shot at a man but
we got homes an' families an' a stake in Texas. You don't
have to be too anxious about us. We'll do our best when
the time comes an' that's about as much as you can expect
from any man. I reckon we ought to be the ones to be
thankin' you." His companions nodded their approval.

"Make yourselves at home and get acquainted. There
isn't much formality around here."

Sul watched them as they moved away and made diffi-
dent attempts to integrate themselves with the Rangers.
Four more guns were better than none. At least he hoped
they were. If they didn't panic and cut and run when the
shooting started. Well, he couldn't worry about that now.
The disappearance of Yancey was a heavy weight on his
mind.

John Drago had sent a message out from Brownsville
by a rider that morning. It didn't add up to much. Such
information as Drago had been able to collect had been
given grudgingly, warily, suspiciously. There had been a
brawl in a river-front cantina. One of the men might have
been Yancey. Everyone was pretty tight-mouthed about
what actually had happened. They didn't want Rangers
turning the district upside down. Anyhow, the one who
could have been Yancey, had been knocked out. A couple
of unidentified men had dragged him outside. That was all
anyone knew or wanted to admit. Sul snorted impatiently.
What the hell kind of trouble had the kid worked himself
into? A fight he could understand. It could happen to
anyone. But, and this was what really worried him, a
cantina ruckus wouldn't account for Yancey's continued
absence. Unless it had ended in murder.

He was scowling at the ground as Pop Warner moved
up beside him. He knew what the old man was going to
say before he spoke.

"No!" Sul's refusal was clipped.

"No what, Sul?" Pop's eyes were blue innocence.

"I can't spare the men to go looking for Yancey. That
was what you were going to suggest, wasn't it?"

"I guess so," Pop admitted. "But you just can't forget about the boy, either. He's not only kin, he's a Ranger. You've always looked after your men. Just because he's your brother doesn't change that."

"If Yancey is in trouble he'll have to get out of it. Word should be coming in from Park and Dewey. Indian Charley is long overdue. Suppose we have to move in a hurry? I can't split up the little force we have to comb along the border for one man."

"I've got a feeling you'd do just that if it wasn't your brother."

Sul had the unhappy feeling that there was a small grain of truth in Pop's rebuke. He was bending over backwards because it was Yancey.

"Maybe just you an' I could go into Brownsville an' then over to Matamoros." Pop made the suggestion hopefully. "We could look around, ask some questions."

"I said no. Do you understand?" The refusal was sharper than Sul intended it to be.

Pop nodded. "I do, Sul. But I've got a feeling you don't.

Chapter Twenty

It was early afternoon on the fourth day out from Matamoros when the wagon trail rolled through a cut in the low hills and came out upon the plateau and the forbidding ranch of Andre Corbel.

Staring at it from his seat on the wagon, Park whistled softly to himself with astonishment. It was the damnedest thing he had ever seen in this or any other part of the country. It seemed to rear out of the very earth itself. Hell, it was no ranch. It was a fortress. No one would ever take it from the outside without the help of artillery. The walls looked as though they were solid blocks of rock.

As he studied the structure, he saw the huge gates swing open. Four men turned their mounts in a fast half-circle and rode out to meet the train.

The lieutenant snapped an order to the drivers and the wagons ground to a halt. He waited, stiff in the saddle, and saluted smartly when Corbel drew near. Then he dropped respectfully just behind the general as Corbel walked his mount the length of the caravan examining each wagon. In passing, his eyes flicked over Yancey but there was no recognition in Corbel's expression. He finished his inspection, wheeled and went back to the head of the column. The train jerked forward again.

From his blouse, the lieutenant drew a sealed paper and passed it to Corbel. The general broke it open, reading carefully and with evident satisfaction.

"The man, Latham," the lieutenant offered the information diffidently, "delivered a prisoner to me. He rides with the second wagon."

Corbel nodded. The presence of the two Rangers interested him more at the moment. He spoke crisply to the officer and the man's eyes widened with astonishment as he listened. Automatically, he glanced back over his shoulder.

Park caught the movement and the surprised question on the lieutenant's face. He knew they had been prompted by something Corbel had said, which could only mean that Corbel, somehow, knew who he and Dewey were. This was trouble, and trouble they weren't likely to survive. He shifted his gun, laying his hand alongside the worn, polished holster. He wondered if Dewey had seen the lieutenant's expression and if it had meant anything to him. Dewey wasn't too sharp at times. A real good man, but not too sharp. He tried to tell himself that his imagination was playing tricks. Corbel couldn't know who they were. If the police chief at Matamoros had known they were Rangers would he have put them on the train? Yep, he admitted dolefully to himself, that was exactly what he would have done. A real cute son of a gun and that was a fact. His admiration for the man's duplicity was tempered by the almost certain knowledge that he and Dewey were in for a going over. There wasn't much he could do about it, either. It was a time to move easy and take things as they came.

Sensing water and an end to the journey, the wagon teams quickened their pace without urging. The gates, which had been closed after Corbel passed through, swung open again and the mounted men trotted through with the wagons and rear guard following. As the gates closed, Park had the dismal sensation of being in prison. He maintained his place in the line as the train wheeled into a crescent and drew to a halt.

With no orders, the drivers stood up and stretched, then dropped heavily to the ground and shuffled toward the well where women were drawing water. Park looped his reins about the brake handle, turned, swung down from the wagon and found himself looking squarely into Corbel's face and the ugly muzzle of a revolver. There were no words, no need for them. This was it for sure. Manning's hand went swiftly for his gun, but he never had a chance. Corbel's bullet caught him full in the face and he died quickly and without a sound. At the report, the drivers and with them the other Ranger, wheeled about. The lieutenant shot Dewey neatly and expertly. The echoes of the reports bounced from wall to wall within the enclosure and were silenced. The bodies sprawled grotesquely in the dirt.

It had happened so quickly that Yancey could only stare incredulously. There had been no time for a cry of warning. He was still too shocked to feel anger.

"We seem to meet in the most unlikely places, Mr. Carter." Corbel edged his horse to the wagon.

Yancey stared at him dumbly. "You never gave them a chance." The words came slowly, dazed.

"My dear sir," Corbel was amused, "are you under the impression that this is some sort of a sporting event? Get down from the wagon, if you please."

The horror of what he had just witnessed was heightened by the indifference of everyone else in the courtyard. After the briefest hesitation, the women continued to draw the water, the drivers reached eagerly for the gourd dippers, a chicken that had squawked indignantly returned to peck in the dirt and a dog scratched himself lazily. Yancey dropped down from the wagon. He felt empty and impotent. Anything he might have said would have been meaningless. The murder had been done. He was probably next.

"I regret that time did not permit a proper execution of your brother's spies. As you will discover, I have a flair for the melodramatic."

"Sul will never let up on you for this." Yancey's voice shook and he was afraid he was going to vomit.

"And who is to tell Captain Carter what happened? You?" Corbel was honestly amused.

He's right, Yancey thought miserably. How will Sul or anyone ever know? He sure isn't going to let me out of here to carry the word back to Texas. He wondered what Corbel was waiting for? Why hadn't they shot him down with Park and Dewey?

As though he understood what was going through the young man's mind, Corbel nodded. "My immediate plans for you may come as something of a surprise. You will be my guest, temporarily. It will be simpler if you will accept my invitation. However, if you make trouble or are difficult I will have you locked up. I am certain you can understand how unpleasant that could become."

"I don't figure it. What do you expect to gain by keeping me here?"

"Ah! Now we come to the kernel of the nut. I am counting on a measure of filial devotion that will bring the Captain Sullivan Carter here when he learns where you are." He was inordinately pleased with himself.

Despite his situation, Yancey laughed, honestly and with pleasure.

Corbel frowned. "You find my explanation humorous?"

"It would be funny if it wasn't so dumb. If you think Sul would move an inch from what he's started out to do to save a brother or his whole family then you don't know him like I do. You're betting on a dead horse, Corbel. If you expect to divert Sul or trade me for a safe passage for your wagons, then you don't know the Rangers. I'm expendable."

For a moment, Corbel scowled and anger flooded his face. Then he shook his head, dismissing Yancey's argument. He didn't believe it. A messenger would be sent that afternoon to take word to the camp on Willow Bend. He could afford to wait a couple of days. He would, also, have time to send news of the wagons to Iron Shirt. Everything would work out nicely. He called to a servant and gave him instructions, indicating Yancey.

"The man will show you to a room. I rely upon your common sense to accept the situation gracefully."

"What about Manning and Dewey? You going to bury them decently or just leave them there on the ground?"

"Naturally, they will be buried." He turned and briskly strode away.

Yancey watched him for a moment, wondering how a shrewd man could be so dumb. Right now he wasn't worried about himself. That would come later, when the pinch was on. He knew Sul, and Sul wouldn't give an inch on a thing like this. So, it was up to him to get out of this fix the best he could. He followed the servant through the semi-darkness of a long passageway to a small bedroom.

When the man had left him, he made brief inspection. There was only one way out of the room and that was through the door. In the wall was a single, barred window but it was higher than a man's head. With his finger tips he tried to pull himself up to look out, but he couldn't make it. Guest or no guest, this was a cell. He threw himself wearily down on the bed and tried not to think of Manning or Dewey. This Corbel was a real tough character and Sul would have to hump himself to catch him.

Chapter Twenty-One

Dusk came quickly near the river. A flight of doves came rocketing out of a *barranca* and passed over Chet Clifton's head with that peculiar whistling sound. The Ranger settled himself a little more comfortably between two concealing rocks and chewed on a piece of dried beef. A distant whippoorwill sounded its call of melancholy.

For a distance of five miles up the river, on the American side, Rangers had concealed themselves at the fording places and throughout the night had waited and watched. Each evening, after the night's guard had been posted, Sul took three or four men and crossed over into Mexico to ride an all-night patrol, scouting miles inland until dawn when they returned to the American side. Somewhere, the wagons and arms were on the move. Sooner or later they would have to make the crossing.

Clifton finished the leatherlike strip of beef and scratched his back against a rock. He wouldn't like to be in Sul's place and have to make his decision. Two days ago, a peon had ridden into Willow Bend and delivered Corbel's message to the Rangers. Sul had listened without comment and then merely nodded his understanding, waiting until the messenger had ridden across the river. Then Sul went back to cleaning his rifle as though nothing had happened. They all knew what he did, but not a man among them was quite sure what he would have done in Sul's place. If he told them they were going to ride against Corbel's place, they would have followed without question.

Clifton pursed his lips in a silent whistle. Sul was going to leave Yancey where he was. They all knew that now. If the kid was in trouble he'd have to get out of it the best he could. The Rangers were not leaving their posts on the river. It was a tough decision for a man to make, but they really hadn't expected Sul to do anything else. They had all lost kin here in Texas. Death was no stranger to them.

Chet tossed a pebble into the water. They weren't going to get any help from Austin. It was up to fifteen or twenty men, unless Drago came with more. They weren't counting on it. A chill wind came winnowing down the river and Clifton shivered against it, drawing an old poncho across his shoulders. It got damn cold at night, cold and lonely. He fingered the rifle lying across his lap.

Without movement, the Indian was a part of the earth on which he flattened himself. He lay with snapping, black eyes boring into the unprotected back of the Ranger. When he inched forward his body glided as soundlessly as a lizard on a wall.

Clifton, brooding upon the water, trying to measure their scanty forces against the unknown and unpredictable, never heard a sound. For a flashing second, before the knife bit deeply into his back, he had a sixth sense of warning, but it was too late. He grunted with a hollow sound and pitched forward. The Indian straightened up and pushed the body contemptuously. For a moment, he stared at it and then stooped swiftly to strip it of revolver, belt, knife and a leather pouch of food. Then the half-naked figure glided away from the river as silently as it had come.

Along the river that night, the scene was repeated. Death came with the feathered whisper of an arrow or the quick, noiseless drive of a knife. In the morning, the sun looked down on the bodies of five Rangers, grotesque in death. Overhead, the buzzards began to gather, sweeping in wide, lowering circles and looking with eager suspicion on what lay below. They rose suddenly as the relief guard of the Rangers came and found the dead men.

They buried the Rangers at Willow Bend. Long after the others had walked silently back to the camp, Pop and Sul stood above the graves.

"All over Texas," Sul's voice grated, "all over Texas little mounds of earth washed away by the rains, cried over by the wind and remembered by no one." He turned almost fiercely upon the older man. "Sometimes I wonder if Texas is worth it."

"You know she is, Sul, or you wouldn't stay."

"I guess so." The broad shoulders drooped wearily. "Five men, friends, I never expected to lose this way. If I could have spared them I would have posted the guards by twos."

"You don't know that would have done any good." Pop turned away with Sul. "Maybe then we would have lost ten instead of five. We're going to take a beating with those wagons anyhow. You know that. So does every man in the troop. We may stop them, but it's going to be expensive."

"We'll stop them, old man. That's what we're here for. Do you expect Texas to pay you a dollar a day for nothing?"

In a circle, the Rangers and the four men John Drago had persuaded to volunteer lounged in moody silence. An open fight would have been different. That they could have understood and accepted. But this silent killing that came without warning and left no trail to follow shook them all. They glanced up at Sul.

"I'm going over into Mexico today, alone. The night rides aren't getting us anywhere. Maybe if I poke around by myself I'll hear or see something. What happened last night can happen again. You can't ease up for a minute. You can't take anything for granted. I don't think the Indians will attack in force. They don't have to if they can get us a few at a time. While I'm away, Pop will be in command. Watch yourselves. I don't want to lose any of you. As soon as I find out anything I'll be back."

Chapter Twenty-Two

Yancey stared bitterly across the room at Anna De Lacey as she sat before the piano. Her fingers rippled with light grace over the keys and the sprightly notes of 'The Minute Waltz' floated from the instrument. The whole thing—Corbel, Anna, the fortress, and his being a prisoner—had about it a sense of complete unreality. Corbel was politely courteous, even solicitous as to Yancey's comfort. He treated Yancey like a guest, chatting enthusiastically at the evening meal of his plans for Texas. Yancey listened incredulously. The man was crazy. He really believed he could get away with it.

Now, Corbel grunted comfortably and heaved himself from a chair. In passing the piano, his hand rested lightly on the top of Anna's head. It was a gesture of possessiveness rather than affection.

" 'The Minute Waltz.' " Corbel smiled at Yancey. "It is an appropriate composition since we have so little time." He bowed. "You will excuse me for a few minutes?"

Alone with Yancey, Anna did not turn from the piano, but her hands dropped away from the keys and rested passively in her lap.

"It would be much simpler if you would tell Andre of your brother's plans." She spoke without facing him. "In the end it would save unnecessary bloodshed. The wagons could be routed to avoid the Rangers and an open fight in which many will be killed."

"In the first place," Yancey snapped the words, "I don't know anything about Sul's plans. And if I did, I sure wouldn't tell Corbel, or you either."

She sighed gently and swung about on the low bench. "Only a child or a very old person can afford the luxury of stubbornness. Those in between must yield a little." She rose then and strolled to one of the narrow windows opening upon the court. The walls loomed high and impregnable, cutting off the country beyond. A crescent moon hung like an ornament just above the parapet. "Come here a moment." She spoke so softly that he barely heard her.

Reluctantly, Yancey stood up and after a brief hesitation moved to stand beside her.

She looked up into his stubborn, set face. "I am fond of you." She made the declaration simply and without affectation. Her face was lovely in the half-light.

"Sure, I know. You're real crazy about me. You also think I'm pretty stupid. Music, moonlight, and Corbel suddenly has to leave the room. I suppose you figure that if I won't tell him what he wants to know I'll tell you."

"That is not why I asked you to come and stand with me."

"Then why? What are you getting at?" He was no longer so positive.

She smiled a little wistfully. "I think it is because in another place and at another time I once stood with such a boy as you in the light of such a moon. It is something I like to remember because I don't think it will ever happen to me again." She strained suddenly upward on tiptoe and brushed his cheek softly with a kiss. "Sometimes I need to recall that I loved and was loved. That is all." She smiled shyly and then the soft huskiness left her voice. "I hope you will not resort to heroics. Andre would be completely unimpressed by them. He is not a gentle man. There are many ways to make you talk and he knows them all. He grows impatient, Yancey."

"I'm not being heroic. I'm just keeping my mouth shut because I don't know anything. He'll have to roll his wagons and take his chances with Sul." He shook his head with a wry and puzzled frown. "You know something? Texas will hang Corbel and, maybe, you. If she doesn't, then Mexico will."

"It is such an undignified way to die, dancing at a rope's end. I have often wondered if it takes very long.

But then," she smiled a secret smile, "like Marie Antoinette, I have such a delicate neck."

He was baffled by her indifference. She genuinely didn't seem to care what happened to her. Corbel's heavy step interrupted his thoughts.

"You must admit, Mr. Carter, we are remarkably indulgent with our prisoners. Rarely, I should think, does a man in your position have the pleasure of such agreeable company." He advanced slowly. "If I do not hear from your brother by tomorrow I shall move out the wagons."

"You're not going to hear from Sul. If I know him, he's written me off the rolls. Did you really think he was going to come here, hat in hand, and dicker with you for me?"

"I intend to put you on the seat of the first wagon," Corbel said slowly. "If Captain Carter attempts to block our crossing, there will be a fight and you will most certainly be shot early in the engagement."

"I can't see how that will do you any good," Yancey said reasonably. "You still won't get the wagons across."

Corbel seated himself and leaned back comfortably. "There is a certain amount of logic in your argument. I must confess, however, that in case you do not prove to be the hostage I hoped for I honestly don't know what to do with you."

"You could turn me loose." Despite his position Yancey almost laughed. If it wasn't so serious this could be a real funny situation.

"I suppose so." Corbel blew speculatively through pursed lips. "I am afraid, though, that I am a man of uncontrollable vindictiveness. It is petty of me, to be sure, but everything else failing, I think I would derive a certain amount of satisfaction in seeing the Rangers shoot another Ranger."

"Andre!" Anna interrupted. There was a note of exasperation in her voice.

"Compassion from you, my dear Anna?" His eyebrows lifted. He was sardonically amused. "I am surprised." He gazed at Yancey. "It is, perhaps, just as well that you do not remain a prisoner for very long, Mr. Carter. You seem to have excited sympathy in a most unexpected quarter."

The girl stared icily at Corbel for a moment and then she wheeled, walking quickly from the room. Lazily, Corbel half-turned his head to watch her.

"A most remarkable and unpredictable woman, Mr. Carter." He waved a hand toward the brandy. "Will you have a drink?"

"I don't want to drink with you, Corbel. You're a murderer and a renegade. Let's stop this play-acting. Maybe it tickles you but it sure doesn't strike me as being funny."

"As you wish." Corbel carefully selected a cigar from the humidor and clipped its end with a small, gold knife. "I only thought to lighten your enforced visit."

"You're amusing yourself, that's all." Yancey turned away and walked through the long corridor and into the large, square patio.

Small fires burned within the court and the huddled figures of men, serapes draped over their shoulders against the chill, were gnomelike in the flickering light. The wagons were still drawn into their crescent, hooded and sinister appearing. At the huge, front gates two guards lounged against the wall, rifles cradled in their arms. This was the only entrance and exit. Yancey's eyes lifted to the high walls. No one could scale them without a ladder. He walked to one of the fires and stood above it, warming his hands. The heads of the drowsing men lifted and eyes regarded him without interest. He wondered what Sul was doing. Sweating it out, probably, trying to out-guess Corbel and the Indians. He looked again at the walls. If there was even half a chance he would take it. A quick run and over. There wasn't a visible handhold on the sheer, vertical surface. Even if he got out, he didn't know where he was or how to get back to Willow Bend.

He turned away from the fire and walked slowly back to the house. Glancing through the open doors of the main *sala* he saw Corbel, still seated in the chair, smoking calmly, his mind fixed upon his mad dream.

"Good night, Mr. Carter." Corbel's back was to him, but he must have heard the step.

A faint, derisive laugh followed him down the passage-way.

Chapter Twenty-Three

           The wagons rolled at daybreak, rumbling through the wide gates. Beside the driver on the lead wagon, Yancey hunched his shoulders against the chill and excitement. This was it. Corbel was going to force a passage somewhere along the river. Within the canvas hood, seated on one of the rifle cases, a sullen guard rocked with the wagon's motion, a gun across his lap. On both sides of the train a mounted detachment of at least fifty men walked their animals to the slow pace of the wagons. The smoke from their cigarettes was blue against the oyster color of the morning. At the head of the column, Corbel rode alone. The crusted gold on his epaulets shone brilliantly in the sun. He was stiff and proud in the saddle.

Yancey stared at him with grudging admiration. He might be a little crazy and a cold killer but he wasn't hiding behind the estancia walls while someone else took the risk with the train. Before he left, Yancey had seen Anna De Lacey only for a moment. She came to the table where he sat alone over hot rolls and coffee and waited until the serving man had filled her cup.

"Don't think too harshly of me." For an instant she leaned forward and her hand covered his.

"I'll do my best not to think of you at all." He dipped a piece of roll into the coffee.

"You don't even try to understand, do you? It is no easy thing to be a woman and alone. I have done what I had to do."

"I'll tell them that when they put a rope around your

neck." He pushed abruptly away from the table and left her there.

Now, he peered out at the barren landscape, leaning forward with elbows on knees, trying to figure a way out of his fix. Behind him the guard nodded drowsily. I could snatch that rifle, he thought. I'd have time for one shot. He glanced at the driver who stared impassively ahead. A holstered gun hung at his right side. With a small, quick movement of his hand Yancey knew he could grab the weapon. Then what? What do I do next? He had a picture of himself bounding across the empty countryside. The horsemen would cut him down before he made a hundred yards. Despondent, he leaned against a wooden rib of the canvas cover and stared ahead.

The peon, in soiled *calzones,* prodded his faggot-laden burro to one side of the road and stood there respectfully as the cavalcade approached. A frayed, coarsely woven straw sombrero was tilted over his face and he half-lifted it in tribute as the wagon train drew near. Corbel and the mounted men ignored him but Yancey stiffened. There was something about the way the peon held himself, even in this humble, obsequious attitude, that caught his attention. For a split second, the face was raised and he caught a glimpse of the sharp, gray eyes set so incongruously in the stained skin. Sul! A broad grin of admiration spread over Yancey's face. I'm a son of a gun. Only Sul would do something like this. He was filled with awe. The odds against Sul and the Rangers were still almost insurmountable but just seeing his brother here filled the young man with confidence. As the wagons passed the solitary figure, Yancey began to whistle cheerfully and the driver turned to regard him with suspicion.

For two days the transport moved steadily northward, halting for a makeshift camp at night and rolling with the first streak of daybreak. Sul had found it easy to follow. The burro and the *calzones* he had bought made an excellent cover. From a distance, one peon looked much like another. So it was no real problem to pretend to be asleep beside the road or swing a machete among the dried stalks of a field. Each time the train passed him, he returned to where he had hidden his horse and, leading the burro, rode ahead to catch it again at a different point. Dressed in the *calzones,* he was somewhat conspicuous astride a horse since peons ordinarily walked or rode a burro. But the few Mexicans he passed looked at him with curiosity and then, apparently, decided he had been lucky enough to steal a horse from someone.

Corbel was following an old cattle trail. It was easier than striking out across the unmarked country. Also, there was water along the way. By now, Sul knew at what point on the river the trail would end. Unless Corbel made a sudden switch in plans, he must bring his wagons to a fording spot some five miles above Willow Bend and attempt the crossing there.

Naked now, Sul stood knee deep in a small stream and scrubbed with handfuls of wet sand at the stain which he had spread on his face, hands and feet. As he washed, he sought desperately for some plan which would allow his few Rangers to overpower Corbel's cavalry. The odds were three or four to one, assuming that there were no armed riders concealed within the hoods of the wagons. He had seen Yancey, so the boy was all right, but he would be on a real hot seat when the fighting started. He hoped his brother would have sense enough to get away during the confusion.

From a blanket roll fastened to the cantle of his saddle he took his boots and clothing and dressed quickly, throwing the *calzones* away. He slapped the burro's flank affectionately. The little animal could take care of itself. Sooner or later some Mexican would find him and marvel at his good luck. He swung himself up into the saddle. His horse was fresh. With luck he could make Willow Bend by nightfall.

As he rode, he wondered about the Indians. If Corbel was smart, and there was no reason to suspect he wasn't, he would keep the savages on the Texas side of the river, throwing them upon the Rangers, while the wagons, virtually unopposed, would cross at the ford. He would like to know if the general and Iron Shirt had agreed on a plan.

The Indian liked to fight in his own fashion. He would have little patience with a white man's talk of strategy. They liked the swift, slashing attack which kept them mobile. They wouldn't understand a holding action to pin the Rangers down. If I only had enough men to hit them first, scatter and keep them off balance, he thought. Putting himself in Corbel's place, he tried to sketch a battle plan for the ford. He would swim his cavalry, if necessary, above and below the shallows and have them sweep down on the flanks of the entrenched Rangers. This would keep the Texans fighting on two sides while the wagons poured across the ford to join the Indians. Everything told him he was facing a nearly hopeless contest in which he was going to lose many men. With a hundred Rangers, he could stop Corbel. With what he had, he could hope for little more than a delaying action which, in the end, would accomplish nothing.

When he reached the river above Willow Bend, the long shadows were gathering over the yellowed countryside, streaking it with dusty blues and purple. He walked his horse into the stream and halted. Dropping from the saddle, he stood calf-deep in the water. The river bottom was rocky and hard, solid enough to carry the weight of the wagons. Corbel would have no trouble here. The teamsters could whip their horses forcing them to run if necessary, without the danger of overturning. The only thing that would slow them down was the slight incline on the Texas side. If the cavalry did its work they wouldn't have to hurry. Once over, the rolling plain would stretch before them.

A faint whistle caused him to look up. From behind a willow clump on the opposite side a man stepped out. Sul recognized him and lifted a hand in greeting. The Ranger strolled down to the river's edge and waited for Sul to cross.

"How you, Cap'n?" The man, Tatum, grinned cheerfully. "You find what you were lookin' for over there?"

"More than I wanted to see. Corbel's moving up with maybe fifty cavalry and I don't know how many armed guards hidden in the wagons. What's happened here? Dewey and Park get back?"

"Nothin' to the first question an' no to the last."

"Then they're in trouble." Sul made no effort to hide his concern.

"Ain't we all." Tatum made the admission with such a cheerful indifference that Sul glanced at him sharply. "I got a relief due soon. If you're a' mind to wait, I'll ride on back to camp with you."

"We can start and meet him on the way. Nothing is going to happen here for two or three days at least. We can pull the guard out for a while." Sul mounted while Tatum went for his horse.

On the way to Willow Bend, Tatum seemed to be enjoying a secret. He whistled with blithe unconcern, darting a glance at Sul now and then and breaking into a pleased grin.

The man's almost idiotic indifference to their situation irritated Sul. "What the devil are you so happy about?"

"Me?" A false innocence spread itself across the Ranger's features. "I'm always good-natured, Cap'n." He chuckled softly to himself.

They met Tatum's relief, Rogers, and the three continued on toward the bend. Every now and then Sul caught the two exchanging sly glances and once they burst into laughter over his serious countenance.

"The two of you are acting like a couple of silly schoolgirls. What's so funny?"

"Who? Us?" they answered in chorus. "Maybe we just ain't got good sense." Tatum whacked Rogers across the back and the men nearly fell from their saddles with laughter.

Sul shook his head. They weren't drunk so there must be another explanation. He had it a few minutes later. At the edge of the Ranger camp at the bend, he pulled his horse up sharply and gazed unbelievingly on the scene.

The small clearing that had served the Rangers at the river now extended for a couple of hundred yards where the underbrush had been hacked away. Two heavy supply wagons were back-ended to the cleared space and sixty or so horses were at a picket line. Small fires dotted the open space. Near the center of the clearing a broad base of coals glowed and above it huge iron kettles simmered. When he had left, there were fifteen Rangers and the four volunteers from Brownsville. Now, he saw, there must be close to seventy-five. While he stared incredulously, one sharp fact registered on his mind. The newcomers were obviously Mexicans. And they seemed to be in easy confederation with the Rangers. Then he saw Don Porfirio.

The man, erect and proud with a smile of welcome on his face, came toward him. They met and Don Porfirio gave Sul the warm *abrazo* of friendship. Then he stepped back and regarded Sul with a twinkle.

"Don Porfirio!" There was astonishment in the greeting. "What are you doing here?"

"The same as you, my friend." The older man's eyes were suddenly grave. "Had there been the time and opportunity, I would have offered our services to you with more formality. As it was, we just came. News, by some mysterious method of transmission, travels quickly. At San Carlos we heard what was happening here and that you had little success in recruiting the help you so badly need. So," he lifted his hands expressively, "I came with my men. We are at your service. I hope you will use us as you see fit."

For a moment, Sul found he was unable to speak. His eyes swept over the scene. Don Porfirio's vaqueros from San Carlos returned his study with quiet, appraising interest. The Ranger felt quick elation. This will do it, he thought. It doesn't give us any edge, but if they'll fight, we can stop Corbel. Something of the question must have shown on his face.

"You are wondering," Don Porfirio's voice was softly rebuking, "whether my men will fight?"

"Corbel has a troop of at least fifty Mexican cavalry riding with him." Sul was reluctant to voice what was in his mind.

"So, you ask yourself if the San Carlos Mexicans will bloody themselves with Andre Corbel's Mexicans? That is it, is it not? The question of Mexican against Mexican?"

"Something like that, Don Porfirio." The confession was made reluctantly.

"I am an American, a Texan." The man was ramrod stiff. "My vaqueros are loyal to me, and most of them are Texas born. Although they are of Mexican extraction, they will fight with me beside you in defense of our homeland."

The statement was made with such simple dignity that Sul felt ashamed. "I am sorry," he said quickly. "I should have known better. Accept my apology if you can."

Together they walked to one of the fires and stood above it, spreading their hands to its warmth. The men watched them silently.

"These are simple men," Don Porfirio said thoughtfully. "They do not have the professional training for warfare that Corbel's men will bring with them. However, it would be a mistake to underestimate their bravery. I have explained to them that it is better to help extinguish this small fire now than to contend with a larger one later. You will tell them what must be done and how we are to do it. They will listen."

Sul drew a deep breath of gratitude. Suddenly, he felt a fierce pride in being a Texan. He studied the faces by the light of the small fires. They were like polished copper in the glow. These alien men had come at the command of their *patron*. They had much to lose and little to gain in such a fight. Few, save the Rangers, would ever remember what they had done. He thought bitterly of the reluctance John Drago had encountered when he tried to enlist the American ranchers.

Slowly, searching for each word carefully, he addressed the San Carlos vaqueros in Spanish. He told them what he knew, what he had seen, the force with which they must contend. He drew no line between Mexicans on one side of the river and Mexican-Americans on the other. He spoke to them as men and Texans. When he had finished, there was silence as they all weighed the situation. Finally, one rose and glanced questioningly at Sul.

"Permiso, Señor?"

Sul nodded, studying the man. There was respect but

no servility in his bearing. He was tough, as they all were, bone lean from long days in the saddle. A machete hung like a sword at his side. When he spoke he did not hurry his words.

"The Indians have broken up their camp in the mountains to the north and come down in small bands. This I know because it was told to me by one whose word I trust. Where they are to gather again and at what time I do not know. But, if we have the time, as you say we do, two or three days before the wagons can reach the river above here, we could attack the small Indian encampments and keep them from reforming."

Sul nodded. The suggestion was valid. If they could catch Iron Shirt's warriors in groups and keep them scattered, the Rangers would be able to protect their rear while they fought the wagon train's cavalry. But there was an almost impossible distance to be covered. Pockets of Indians would be spread over the rolling countryside. They could spend months trying to pry them out of their hiding places.

He explained this carefully, with a sensitive regard for the vaquero's pride, and saw that the man nodded understandingly, accepting his words with solemn evaluation.

"We will make a plan." Sul addressed himself only to the San Carlos men. His own Rangers needed no reassurance. "We will decide, all of us together, on what is best and then we will do it."

There was a quick nodding of heads and an exchange of glances. The gringo was treating them as fighting men of responsibility and not as ignorant peons taken from the fields. They would trust him.

Night lay like a dark scarf along the river. Within the clearing, earthenware pots of frijoles bubbled and dried chilies were crumbled into the beans to give them strength. In the blackened iron kettles freshly slaughtered beef simmered in a hardy stew. Tortillas were scorched quickly over the coals, twisted and dipped into the pots. Under the spell of a common cause the normal constraint between Anglo and Mexican in Texas vanished. Ranger and vaquero squatted side by side, talked haltingly, sharing food and tobacco. Later, a guitar and an accordion were brought out and old songs were played.

Sitting beside Sul, Don Porfirio listened and watched. "It would be a good thing," he mused aloud, "if together we could plant a small seed of understanding here between the Texans and those of Spanish and Mexican blood. I am afraid, though, it will take a long time maturing. There are too many prejudices and suspicions that grow like weeds to choke it off."

Sul drew thoughtfully on his twisted cigarette. He was still marveling over this unexpected addition to the small force of Rangers. Corbel must never suspect their presence. The San Carlos men must be moved from the bend and out of sight from the opposite shore. Fanning out from the upper ford, the most likely crossing place, there was a thick belt of blackjack oak and chaparral in which the volunteers could be hidden. This would serve a double purpose, covering the Rangers at the river from an Indian attack and still having them close enough to lend assistance at the ford if it was needed. He would make the move tomorrow. With a start, he realized that Don Porfirio was still speaking.

"My roots will go deep in this land." An almost shy smile illuminated the older man's features. "I am to be a father, my friend. A father at my age. What do you think of that?"

Sul reached over to take Don Porfirio's hand. "Congratulations. How is Dona Marguerita?"

"Complacent, after the manner of a woman who secretly believes she has accomplished this miracle by herself." Don Porfirio chuckled. "Still, she pretends it is nothing while I feel an almost irresistible desire to strut and crow. To have a son born here in my adopted country. That is something, my friend."

Secretly, Sul wished there was some way he could keep the man from the fighting which must come. He had too much at stake now to risk his life. He thought of and discarded half a dozen arguments. The smallest suggestion that Don Porfirio return to San Carlos, leaving his men with the Rangers, would be an insult which would breach their friendship forever. He abandoned the idea reluctantly.

With an apology, he rose and left to check the posting of a guard, dividing the night between Don Porfirio's men and the Rangers. This was only a normal precaution. He didn't actually expect an assault here. When he was satisfied that the camp was in order, he rolled himself in a blanket and, making a headrest of his saddle, bedded down for the night.

Heavy on his mind was the fate of Park Manning and Dewey. For Yancey, he felt a paternal anger. If Corbel wanted to dispose of him, he would have done it long ago. Yancey's presence with the train meant that he was still comparatively safe. He still couldn't figure how the boy had blundered into Corbel's hands. Park Manning and Dewey were something else. Whatever had happened to keep them from reporting back, had been swift and final. Mentally he drew another circle with crayon on the map back at headquarters. He lay for a long time, staring up at the sky. Finally, he slept.

Chapter Twenty-Four

The first graying of dawn was smeared against the sky. A mounted man on the Mexican side of the river sat motionless as he looked through a glass at the Willow Bend encampment. This was the second morning he had appeared at almost the same hour. Sul and the Rangers watching him were pressed flat upon the ground, wrapped in their blankets as though still asleep.

There was no mistaking the figure of Andre Corbel. He had come to see for himself that the Texans were still encamped at the bend. Some ten miles behind him, the wagons waited. They would move during the night and in the morning, at daybreak, he would force a crossing at the ford up the river. He telescoped his glass and put it in a leather case. The tactics of the Rangers disturbed him. Carter, he thought, must know he would not attempt to drive the train at this spot. Why, then, did they remain here? Because he could find no ready answer to the question, it plagued him. He dismissed the notion that Sullivan Carter was not aware of the train's movement. He must have done what he, Corbel, would have done in his place, send a scout or scouts into Mexico. So, he was fully aware of what was happening. Why, then, this apparent indifference to the situation? He turned his horse and allowed it to walk, retracing the route he had traveled, while he tried to solve the puzzle.

When the rider across the river had passed from sight, Sul rolled out of his blanket and stood up. Around him the Rangers stretched, scratched themselves, yawned and went to the river to splash their faces and rinse the sleep from their mouths. They were edgy with the waiting.

Over the tin cups of scalding coffee, they listened without expression as Sul spoke.

"We'll move tonight. Kramer," he addressed one of the men, "you stay behind. Build a few small fires and keep them burning in case Corbel or one of his men comes back for a look. I want them to think we're still here. The rest of us will pull out at sundown."

The hours of the day dragged interminably and the tension mounted. The men sat apart from each other, honing knives already sharpened to a razor's edge. They cleaned and re-cleaned rifles, checked ammunition endlessly or just squatted and stared across the river. By mid-afternoon the strain of inactivity was almost unbearable. Tempers snapped and there was a sudden, explosive fight over the accidental upsetting of a coffee pot. The two men slugged at each other with heavy grunts. There was no fury in the contest and Sul made no attempt to halt it nor did any of the other Rangers step in to separate the contestants. It ended as quickly and as illogically as it had started. Bruised, bleeding from mouth and nose, clothing torn, their breath coming in heavy, exhausted gasps, the pair faced each other and grinned sheepishly.

"What're we doin' this for?"

"Dogged ef Ah know."

"Let's cut it out then."

"Suits me."

Suddenly there was laughter. The men exploded with it, rolling on the ground and punching playfully at each other. The fight had cleared the air. They sprawled now in easy, indolent attitudes. Someone brought out a greasy deck of cards and a poker game was started on a spread blanket. They could wait now. Sul smiled to himself. He knew his men. That was why he had let the two fight it out. They were the safety valve for them all.

The Indians had come down from the hills. They were grouped over the rolling plain, concealed by the low, sweeping rises. Iron Shirt had listened carefully to the messenger who had come from Corbel. It was the white man's order that they attack in the morning. The chief nodded without comment. He was seeking a plan that would put the wagons and the arms into his hands without sending his warriors to Corbel's assistance. The man had bled the Indians of thousands of cattle. The guns should be theirs without fighting. Suppose he held back and let the white men fall upon each other? No. That would not accomplish anything. He must, at least, make a token show of aiding Corbel. Reluctantly, he abandoned the pleasant idea of treachery. Later, with his braves well armed, he could deal with Corbel.

Hands clasped behind his back, Andre Corbel walked the length of the wagon train, inspecting each cumbersome vehicle. There must be no weakness of wheel or axle, team or driver, to hold them up at the river. The crossing must be fast and complete. Nothing could be left to chance. He could count on his mounted troops. He paid them well, treated them with respect. They were disciplined and would carry out their orders. The drivers and the guards within the wagons were something else. They were the riffraff of a border town, the scum of prisons in Vera Cruz, Victoria and Monterrey. These would have to be lashed forward when the fighting started. He had instructed the lieutenant of the cavalry to cut down the first man who made an attempt to abandon his wagon.

He halted beside one of the wagons and studied Yancey Carter. The boy returned his gaze mockingly.

"I keep wondering why I do not have you shot, Mr. Carter."

"I've been puzzling over that myself." Yancey had accepted his situation with a philosophy that had surprised him. He was here. He was stuck with it.

"I bear you no personal animosity. I'm sure you must appreciate that. In the beginning, I thought you might have been of some small value to me. I was mistaken, and since the error in judgment was mine I do not hold you to blame."

"That's real generous of you, sir." Yancey regarded him with a wide-eyed innocence.

"In the morning, you will have the privilege of being a spectator while history is made. Providing of course, that one of your brother's Rangers does not shoot you from that seat there."

"General," Yancey said emphatically. "I'm going to get back and lie down in that wagon or, if I get a chance, cut out and run for it."

"I can't say I blame you, Mr. Carter." The man nodded and passed on while Yancey looked after him with puzzled wonder. Maybe he was crazy, but the magnitude of his hallucination commanded a certain respect.

Yancey leaned against the wagon and idly watched while a hot, iron tire was hammered to fit the rim of a wheel. Because his situation had in it an element of the ridiculous he found himself unable to take it as seriously as he should. A hostage without value, a prisoner no one particularly wanted.

He indulged himself with fancied acts of heroism. He could creep among the wagons at night, and with the casks of powder, blow up the train. He could snatch a revolver from the teamsters and shoot Corbel. He could stampede the horses and, with this single act, dismount the cavalry. He would be known as the man who prevented an Indian uprising and saved Texas. He grinned to himself. That was all kid stuff. Nevertheless, he had a small suspicion that Sul, in a similar spot, would do something. I guess, he told himself moodily, I'm not a real, first-class hero. The idea depressed him. A great opportunity was somewhere at hand but he wasn't sure what it was. It was mighty discouraging.

Watching from the thick fringe of oak and scrub, Don Porfirio and the vaqueros saw the first of the Indians. They appeared silently, a dozen or more topping a ridge a half a mile or so away. They were drawn there against the lowering sun as though cut from dark paper and pasted on a crimson background. For perhaps ten minutes, the group held their ponies motionless and then they wheeled and vanished as mysteriously as they had appeared.

Don Porfirio turned to Sul. "This is all new to me, Captain. What do you make of it?"

"I think Iron Shirt just wanted to look things over. Maybe he knows you're here, maybe not. Anyhow, they won't attack at night. The chances are that Corbel and the old chief have been sending runners back and forth and that the general wants an Indian assault at the same time he starts the push with his wagons. That should be in the morning. Things are likely to get pretty hot around here, Don Porfirio, even before the sun rises."

The man of San Carlos shook his head. "It would seem to me that this situation is one for the Army to meet and not the business of the Texas Rangers."

"It is." Sul made the admission cheerfully. "The Army is empirical, Don Porfirio. It only believes what it can see. I couldn't show it anything."

They walked back into the sheltering thicket. No attempt at a camp had been made. This was an outpost with men and horses ready. The vaqueros squatted on their heels, smoking and talking quietly. No fires had been laid. They ate cold meat and tortillas taken from greasy, leather pouches.

Beside his horse, Sul turned to the older man. "There's no way of knowing how many braves Iron Shirt has hidden back there. He won't commit them all at once but when they come, they'll come running. That is how you'll have to meet them, horse to horse. I have a feeling Iron Shirt hasn't much stomach for this fight. He might break it off in the face of real opposition."

"What about you, my friend, you and your handful of Rangers?"

Sul shrugged. "We'll do the best we can."

"That is usually good enough, is it not, Captain?" Don Porfirio made the statement with quiet confidence and then stepped back, lifting a hand. "Go with God, Ranger."

At the ford the Rangers had spaced themselves out along the bank that commanded the crossing. The ledge was strewn with rocks and boulders and afforded some natural cover. Where it was lacking, the men had tugged and hauled the stones into place. They tested the scattered fortifications, each in his own way and to his own satisfaction. They crouched or lay flat upon their bellies, sighting down their rifles, measuring the distance across the river, holding an imaginary driver on the bead and squeezing the trigger. They had already counted the odds against them. Three to one here at the ford with the San Carlos vaqueros to hold and protect their rear. It all depended now on how Corbel had planned the crossing and whether the Indians would break through Don Porfirio's riders.

"There are sure enough a lot of 'ifs' in this, ain't there, Cap'n?" Young John Kendricks rolled to his side and glanced up at Sul who stood, looking speculatively across the river. "If they cross here. If that there cavalry splits up and comes from two directions. If the Indians don't break out. It's real iffy, I'd say." He grinned. "If I had my druthers I druther be someplace else."

As always, Sul found himself mildy surprised by the philosophy of these men Texas called her Rangers. They were, he thought, no braver than most. Like most people, they came from simple backgrounds where life and death were measured by a span of years rather than by the flash of a gun. Yet, they had developed a stoic acceptance of duty, and duty they did. He dropped down to the ground and rested his back against a rock that was still warm from the sun. There was no need to walk among the men, cautioning, counseling. They knew what must be done and each in his own way would do his part. He settled back gratefully. The twilight would be brief and the night soon upon them. He glanced up as Pop Warner stooped beside him.

"You'll be scratching with your pen for a month trying to write up the report of this one, old man." Sul studied the grizzled face. "Why don't you go home?"

"With all the money I'm making here?" Pop simulated astonishment. "A man would be a fool to quit a real good job like this one."

"I always figured you just stuck around for the money." Sul thrust a tongue into his cheek.

"Mercenaries have a fixed place in the battles of history. Would you deny me mine?"

"I wouldn't rob you of a minute of it, old man." Sul grinned at him and then sobered. "You take care of yourself, hear?"

Pop passed him a ragged plug of tobacco and Sul bit off a piece, working it into a soft ball. They chewed contentedly, each finding an unspoken pleasure in the other's company. Sul glanced at the sky from beneath the lowered brim of his hat. Already the first of the stars were pricking at the night. There was nothing more to do. This was the Army all over again. You waited. He slid down the rock a little and closed his eyes.

He awoke once during the night and discovered that a blanket had been drawn over him. "You're an old woman, Pop," he mumbled sleepily and wondered, as he so frequently did, about these lean, reckless and hard-bitten men. They, whose spare lives had so little softness in them, frequently displayed a surprising gentleness toward each other.

It seemed only a few minutes after he had closed his eyes again when he was drawn from sleep by the insistent tugging of a hand on his shoulder. He jerked upright and looked around. All down the thin line the men were being awakened, prodded by the boot of the watch. They grunted or cursed flatly without emphasis or emotion, pulled themselves to their feet and stood staring across the river which lay beneath a light, writhing mist.

The sky in the east held the dingy color of an oyster shell. In the clear, thin air of the morning, the men heard the first, distant creak of wagon wheels. The sound was sharply distinct and it riveted them to their positions. They were fixed in crouching attitudes over a small fire. Others stood with steaming tins of black coffee or held their teeth on a strip of raw bacon. Then, without haste, the fire was scattered and stamped out, the coffee drunk. Hands reached for rifles propped against the rocks. No one spoke, not through caution, but because there was nothing to say. The time of waiting was over. The day and what it held was upon them.

The minutes slid away, and the sounds of morning asserted themselves with the excited chatter of a squirrel, the cawing of a distant crow, the rasping, angry cry of a blue jay. The screeching progress of the wagons was clearer now. The listening men could hear the sharp report of a whip as it curled out over the backs of a laboring team. The Rangers were flat on the ground behind the low shelter of the rocks, peering through the cracks, eyes straining for the first sign of movement on the opposite bank. Here and there a man licked at dry lips or, with an unconscious gesture of nervousness, ran a hand over chin and cheek. The Rangers wriggled chest and belly against the hard dirt as though to burrow deeper into it. Although their eyes were fixed ahead, their ears were alert for a sound behind

them, a sound they expected but did not want to hear—
the high, fierce screaming of the Indians as they bore
down upon the San Carlos vaqueros guarding their rear.
If Iron Shirt was going to attack, it would be now.

Within a shallow fold of the low, rolling slopes, Iron
Shirt sat upon his pony and waited. Strung out on both
sides of him were close to a hundred mounted warriors.
They were stripped of all non-essentials. This was no
display of color and barbaric pageantry. They were
fighting men and eager for the kill. A few had guns. The
others were armed with bows and arrows, long deadly
lances, heavy clubs to which sharpened stone heads had
been attached.

They sat their restive ponies, holding them with soft
clucking sounds, and glanced at Iron Shirt, waiting for the
word. The chief was restraining them with difficulty. He
wanted to hear the first of the shots which would tell them
that Corbel had engaged the Rangers. Then, and only
then, would he drive to the attack. Behind him, concealed
within a second, stubbled trough, was a reserve force of
almost a hundred braves. With difficulty and long argument, Iron Shirt had prevailed with this strategy. This was
not the way the tribes would have fought. Left to themselves they would have flung the entire force across the
heaving plain in overwhelming numbers. Iron Shirt
wanted more than the destruction of the Rangers. He
wanted Corbel, also. He had explained his plan to the
headmen of the different tribes who had sent warriors to
join him. With the first attack, he would seemingly join
Corbel in exterminating the small force of Rangers. Then,
with the wagons safely across the river, Corbel's forces
decimated, weary and in confusion from the attack at the
ford, the second wave of Indians would fall upon the
Mexican troops. With this single, master stroke of treachery, they would have the wagons and their precious car-
goes and destroy the greedy man who had demanded and
received thousands of stolen cattle in payment for the
arms. Once the headmen and warriors had understood the

measure of Iron Shirt's duplicity they had applauded it in silence, their bright eyes snapping. It would be done as he had said.

Hidden by the thin woods, the mounted men of San Carlos faced the empty plain. It heaved and rolled before them as though the sea had once passed here and the waves frozen into the dun-colored hills and small valleys. They had seen nothing, heard nothing, but they knew the Indians were there and would come.

Above, climbing cumbersomely in the still heavy air which as yet provided no sweeping currents, the buzzards worked their way higher and higher. Their eyes were fixed on the ground and the strange tableau which was laid out there. They, also, had to wait.

Along the river, the Rangers stared unbelievingly at the opposite bank and, for a moment, could not believe what was happening there.

"Now this here," one of the men spoke for them all, voicing what the troop felt, "I just don't believe even though I'm a-lookin' straight at it."

As though they were in parade formation, moving unhurriedly and in perfect alignment, the Mexican cavalry drew up on the easy slope of the shore. General Andre Corbel, resplendent in full uniform, rode at the center and slightly ahead. The line halted while the general, hands folded on his saddle, studied the ford, the Texas bank. The disciplined ranks held motionless. Behind them, separated by a couple of hundred yards, the wagons ground to a halt in a column of twos.

Studying the formation, Sul pursed his lips and blew soundlessly through them. No man who had ever soldiered, not even one of such consummate vanity as Andre Corbel, would display his forces before the opposition in such a manner. It was the act of a madman, a monumental gesture of contempt for the Rangers. He must know they were waiting. Yet, everything about his position indicated that he was determined to drive straight ahead, take his casualties and overwhelm the entrenched Texans with one, irresistible assault.

"You reckon he's waitin' for a brass band?" A Ranger raised the dry question and there was a faint, rippling chuckle down the line. "Do you really think he's a-goin' to try it this way, Cap'n?"

"It sure looks like it." Sul still had difficulty in accepting this overwhelming display of conceit. "We'll know soon enough."

The seconds ticked by, measured by the heavy breathing of the waiting men. This was too much luck. There must be a trick in it somewhere.

Andre Corbel, his face set rigidly toward the Texas shore, drew his sword.

"Ah'll jus' be dogged-damned," a Ranger whispered, awestruck. "Ef they blow a bugle now Ah'm goin' to cut an' run foah it because you suah can't fight no crazy man." He voiced what was in every Ranger's mind. There was something eerie in the spectacle and it made them uneasy.

For a second, Corbel held his sword aloft. The first sunlight touched the blade. Then he swept it downward and kicked cruel spurs into his horse. The wave of mounted men swept forward, racing down the easy slope. Behind them, with frantic yells, the teamsters laid heavy whips upon the startled teams, beating them with an insane fury and the wagons jolted forward, gathering momentum in a desperate effort to keep within the shield of charging cavalry.

The troops hit the water with a lacy curtain of spray which hid them for a moment. Then, they drove through it with such a display of recklessness and superb horsemanship that the Rangers almost forgot their deadly mission. Then they fired.

The first blast cut through the charging cavalry as a gust of wind might lay open a path in a field of high grass. Horses reared skyward, pitching dead and wounded men high into the air. A sudden scream, high, lonely and desperate, slashed at the morning, and the air was scented by the sweetly acrid odor of burnt powder. In the middle of the shallow river there was a confused tangle of men

and animals. The Rangers shot unhurriedly, with coldly
dispassionate accuracy that threw the disorganized cavalry
back with a shock, nailing them to the stream. Then the
wagons, great lumbering engines of destruction, the teams
whipped to a runaway frenzy were bearing down on the
trapped troopers. As wildly improbable things happen in
a dream, the Rangers stared at the impossible, screaming
water—water writhing fury. Two of the plunging wagons
locked wheels in a splintering crash that ripped out their
axles and sent them careening on their sides in the water—
water dyed scarlet by the blood of men and animals.

Corbel, a raging maniac now, slashed wildly with his
sword at the bewildered and reluctant troopers in a last
effort to drive them on. He screamed an order and a
frightened trooper thrust his pistol into the contorted
mouth. The slug tore Andre Corbel's face away. Without
order now, wanting only to escape the fire of the Rangers
they could not see, the mounted men who remained spun
their horses away, some clawing for the Mexican shore,
some stumbling their mounts downstream. From the tails
of the wagons, the guards flung away their guns and
dropping into the water, ran ashore to the concealment
and safety of the brush. Stunned and in a hopeless tangle,
the drivers leaped down and ran.

Yancey, clutching for support at the tumbling cases and
casks within the wagon, saw the driver rise and prepare to
jump. A bullet caught the man with the soft-thud of a
ripe melon being struck. He fell, the reins trailing from his
lifeless hands, while the maddened team tore out at an
oblique angle for the Texas shore, slamming up and over
the bank and through the massed catclaw that ripped at
their flanks and added to their panic. Yancey crawled
forward in the hope of retrieving the reins but they trailed
and whipped on the ground beyond his reach, snapping
and flying upward like lunatic serpents. He clutched at the
smooth seat to save himself from being pitched out. The
wheels hit a stone and flew into the air, slamming to the
ground. There was no holding the team, now, even if
Yancey could have reached the reins. He braced himself
to ride it out.

From behind their protective rocks, the Rangers raised themselves to stare with silent wonder at the wreckage below and the fleeing men on horse and afoot. They didn't even bother to shoot at the scrambling targets. Up and down the stream the bodies lay half-submerged. Shattered and overturned wagons littered the ford. Above and below the Rangers' post some of the teams had come to a halt and were waiting with heaving docility for a familiar command or a hand on the reins. The carnage was so complete and had been achieved so quickly that the Texans regarded each other with dumb amazement. There hadn't been a casualty among them and very little effort exerted but they found themselves breathing heavily.

Iron Shirt and his braves had listened to the sound of gunfire from the river. Yelling triumphantly they drove heels into the lean flanks of their skittish ponies. They screamed as they rode, working themselves up to a pitch of excitement that carried them up over the brow of the shallow ravine in a single wave. The drumming of hooves beat out an accelerated cadence and the dust rose behind them in a trailing cloud.

Then, meeting the Indians head on, the men of San Carlos drove to break the assault.

For a second, surprise checked the fanatical screams of the Indians. This was opposition they had not counted on, a thundering line of men who were not spending themselves with the firing of rifles or pistols. Machetes, secured by a thong at the wrist, sparkled in the early sun. The vaqueros bore them like sabers. Then the lines met with a dull crash, horse against horse, man against man. At this locked range, the bows and arrows of the Indians were useless. Those with old muskets fired them at point-blank range. Along the line there were screams of pain as a San Carlos man was hit or a body was pitched from its saddle. Then in a swirling, eddying fight that spun like a whirlpool on the plain, the machetes were at work. They rose and fell, slashing and cutting, splitting skulls, ripping terrible wounds into bare chests.

"*Mano y mano!*" Hand to hand. The defiant yell from the vaqueros answered the savage screams.

Indian and vaquero fought in single combat. They struggled in groups of twos and threes. Don Porfirio, his face a bloody mask from a glancing cut on his cheek, stood up in his stirrups and drove the machete down upon the shaven head of a brave who came at him, low over the side of his pony, with fixed lance. The force of the impact threw them both from their horses. Don Porfirio's body was half-covered by that of the dead Indian as the battle surged away. Then the Indians suddenly broke off the engagement, wheeling their mounts without command and racing back across the plain, leaving their dead and wounded to lie with the shapeless humps of San Carlos' casualties. The Indians fled, yelling their fury and outrage, daring the vaqueros to follow. They disappeared behind a shallow ridge.

The Rangers, mounted now, came up from the river in a tight group. They were too late to see the bloody conflict in which the men of San Carlos had met and broken the Indian attack. They saw only the dotted plain, the riderless horses. And they saw a driverless wagon as it careened toward the ravine into which the Indians had vanished.

With the canvas of its top bellying out like a sail, the wagon was a grotesque ship upon a static sea, pulling out fully half a mile ahead of Don Porfirio's men as the Rangers joined them.

In the wagon, bruised and half-dazed by the beating he had taken from pitching cases and casks, Yancey felt the pace of the team slacken. The animals were spent from the wild run. They stumbled along blindly, their sides lathered and heaving. Yancey peered from the canvas tunnel and saw a solitary Indian appear suddenly on the ridge. Turning, he could see the distant mass of the San Carlos men and the Rangers as they started to move forward cautiously in the direction of the stalled wagon.

Sul wanted the wagon and its contents. At least, he didn't want it captured by the Indians who were undoubtedly still gathered in the ravine. Yet, there were the wounded of San Carlos to be taken care of. Some twenty

of the vaqueros were on the ground. A few crawled pitifully, mute in their death agony. Others lay where they
had been flung, faces buried in the dirt or sightless eyes
turned upon the buzzard-filled sky. The Rangers had
found Don Porfirio, badly hurt but still alive. With a hand
signal, Sul checked the advance of his men and the remaining vaqueros. The survivors were too weary to be led
into an ambush he felt certain must lie over the rim of the
slope.

Yancey stared at the solitary, mounted Indian ahead.
Then the watcher was joined by a second and a third.
More appeared until twenty-five or so were gathered in a
dark, watchful line. For some reason they held back.
Maybe, Yancey thought hopefully, they think it is some
sort of a trap. If I lie doggo they may go away. Then the
idea came to him that he himself could use the wagon as a
trap. With the butt of a rifle that the guard had abandoned, he stove in the heads of the powder casks and
working backward to the wagon's tail, laid a long, loose
trail of the black grains. He kept glancing forward through
the arched opening of the wagon's top. The Indians were
walking their horses, leaning forward and studying this unexpected prize. Then they divided, approaching from
two sides with animal caution. They drew up and held
what seemed to be a wordless consultation.

Concealed behind the jumble of casks and cases,
Yancey watched. He held a long, drip-headed match in
his fingers, poised on the surface of a rough board. There
was just a chance, he told himself, that he could get away.
It was slim, but if he didn't go through with what he had
in mind he was a dead duck, anyhow. Maybe in the
confusion he could escape. That was as far as he could
get. Maybe. He didn't want to be a hero. All he wanted
was to create what the text books at military school had
called a diversionary action.

The Indians had halted again, considering the wagon.
Then, with a sudden whoop of pleased excitement, they
kicked their ponies into action and swept forward.

Yancey struck the match and it burst into yellow flame.

He touched it to the end of the snake-like fuse and threw himself from the wagon. He ran, bent over, weaving and twisting with the agility of a jack rabbit.

Watching from a distance, Sul, the Rangers and the men of San Carlos saw the Indians as they closed in a tight circle about the wagon. They watched the bounding figure of the unknown runner as it raced toward them. Then, as the ring of mounted savages closed in to obscure the wagon from view, a great, fiery blossom erupted as the load of powder exploded within the closed ranks of the Indians.

Terribly burned by the furious blast, reeling back with anguished howls of pain, their lank, greasy hair on fire and their seared skin hanging in stinking patches from their tortured bodies, the Indians were hurled from pain-maddened ponies which bolted in all directions. The savages rolled on the ground tearing at each other in blind agony.

One buck, who had been on the outside of the ring caught the furnace-like blast from a distance. The flash half-blinded him but, in the moment of terror, he saw the running figure as it raced for safety. Bending low over the horse, which ran as much in fear as from its rider's urging, the Indian held the long, deadly lance waist high. Over his own, gasping breath, Yancey could hear the dull pounding of his pursuer. He dared not look back, not wanting to lose a second of his pitifully small advantage. He strained toward the group of horsemen who were driving their mounts to his rescue.

Sul and the Rangers yelled their encouragement. It didn't matter who the man was, one of Corbel's guards or a driver. He had fired and destroyed the wagon, and they wanted to help him now.

The lance caught Yancey below the shoulder blade, driving in with terrible force. As the boy fell, the Indian, still clinging to the shaft, was pulled from the straining horse and pitched high into the air. He broke his neck in falling and was dead beside his victim as the Rangers drew up.

Sul Carter bent and looked long into the face of his brother. Then, gently, as though he was fearful of causing pain, he pulled the lance out and with silent fury broke the shaft across his knee.

There was no fight left in the Indians. Those who had survived the explosion withdrew in stoic silence. Within the shallow ravine, Iron Shirt tried to urge the remaining braves to an attack upon the Rangers. They turned away from him and departed in small groups. They were men of many tribes and owed him no allegiance. The old chief watched them go, the bitter taste of failure in his mouth.

Beside the river, within the damp coolness of the willows, the Rangers buried the dead of San Carlos and with them Yancey Carter. They lay, unmarked, beside the five Rangers who had been killed at their sentry posts.

Sul stood among the little mounds and wept. All over Texas. The phrase recurred to him. Little mounds of earth, cried over by the wind. He thought of something he had said to Park Manning: "Kid brothers never grow up."

He bent down and smoothed the edge of the damp mound that was his brother's grave. His fingers rested there for a moment, then trailed away as they might in fondly touching a cheek for remembrance. Then he walked away and did not look back.

They returned Don Porfirio to San Carlos, swung in a hammock-like litter between two horses. The old man managed a wan smile later when he looked up from his bed into the faces of Sul and Dona Marguerita.

"We fought well, Captain?" He asked the question softly.

Sul nodded and took the outstretched hand. "You fought well, Don Porfirio."

The old man sighed. "Then, perhaps, we may not have to do it again tomorrow. *Verdad?*" He paused. "Such a big price to pay for a madman's dream."

The thin line moved at a slow walk down the dusty main street of Davis toward the adobe headquarters, and youngsters at their play stopped to watch them pass. A few persons stood in the narrow doorways, shading their eyes against the sun's glare. They counted, from long habit, the number returning against the number that had ridden away. And, as always, they found it less.